I BELIEVE IN MIRACLES
Containing
Pearls of Great Price

Rebekkah Clark

Bloomington, IN authorHOUSE Milton Keynes, UK

AuthorHouse™
1663 Liberty Drive, Suite 200
Bloomington, IN 47403
www.authorhouse.com
Phone: 1-800-839-8640

AuthorHouse™ UK Ltd.
500 Avebury Boulevard
Central Milton Keynes, MK9 2BE
www.authorhouse.co.uk
Phone: 08001974150

First published by AuthorHouse 6/19/2006

ISBN: 1-4259-3506-0 (sc)

Printed in the United States of America
Bloomington, Indiana

This book is printed on acid-free paper.

rebekkahclark@btinternet.com

WRITE A BOOK

I've had many requests over the years to set down in writing some of my many amazing experiences as I have walked with the Lord.

The first came from an administrator working with the Billy Graham Organisation. At my initial training interview, the worker encouraged me to write, after listening to my testimony and the recounting of a few tales!

My sanguine personality is that of an entertainer. So telling these accounts has been easy. The harder part has been to present this to you in written form. For that I am extremely grateful to dear friends who have scribed for me. That's *their* gifting. Also many thanks to my husband who has helped me with the final draft. We need each person to play his or her part.

My prayer is that this book will be a real blessing and encouragement to you and that it will challenge you to tap in to your own God-given potential as you step out in faith, believing that you too have heard the Lord's voice.

Rebekkah Clark was brought up in North West London, the middle child of three, with an older sister and a younger brother. She became a Christian at the age of eighteen and met her husband shortly afterwards. They reside in the Home Counties, England and have three daughters and seven grandchildren.

ACKNOWLEDGEMENTS

I would like to thank the many people who have encouraged me to write this book and who through their enthusiasm and dedication have ensured that even when problems have arisen, I have not given up.

I should also like to thank those who have been involved in the typing, computer processing and reading of the various drafts and, in particular, Matt Lawrence (**www.mattart.co.uk**) for the design on the front cover and for the illustrations throughout the book.

Finally, I should like to thank the many people who allowed their stores to be told. These stories demonstrate that God is interested in every part of our lives and is eager to bless and intervene to our benefit if we allow Him to be involved.

Rebekkah Clark
rebekkahclark@btinternet.com

VISIT OUR WEBSITE
www.lifechangingbooks.org

Also available thereon:
Heaven - Can I Be Sure? - Can it Be Lost? By Peter Smails
Being convinced that the Bible teaches that once saved, always saved, author Peter Smails looks at all of the verses that seem to say the opposite, to see what they really are saying.

I BELIEVE IN MIRACLES

Chapter 4
MUSICAL INTERLUDE

Chapter 5
NEEDS SATISFIED

Chapter 6
ANGELIC ENCOUNTERS

Chapter 7
YOU SHALL BE FREE INDEED

Chapter 8
USING THE GIFTS

Chapter I

NEW BEGINNINGS

It happened to me

I surrender all

When Billy Graham came to town

Reaching out

This is church folks

The lover of my soul

Childlike faith

God is interested in even the simple things

IT HAPPENED TO ME: MY PERSONAL EXPERIENCE

"For I know the plans I have for you," declares the Lord, "plans to prosper you and not to harm you, plans to give you hope and a future." (Jeremiah 29 v 11 NIV)

I was not to know just how much this verse was to mean to me. I had come from what I thought was a loving family home. Of course there were problems but I thought that was just part of normal everyday living. I knew nothing then of dysfunctional families!

I was in my teens and circumstances in my upbringing had brought me to a place where I was very down, to the extent that I was contemplating ending my life. I took the bus to town and walked along to the railway station, with every intention of jumping in front of an oncoming train.

That would put an end to my heartache, loneliness and feelings of rejection, because I felt I was not loved.

I was walking towards the station when a man stopped me – and told me that Jesus *loved* me! I found what he said very hard to believe in the mental mess I was in. The man was not easily put off. He persisted in telling me how much Jesus cared for me, why He'd even laid down His own life for *my* sin. Someone dying for me *because* He loved me, when I was wanting to die because I thought nobody *did!* It shook me to the core. I was not in the mood for small talk and yet these words began to penetrate the aching void within me and I found myself listening as the man said that Jesus so wanted me to receive His abundant life! It *had* to be better than I had known up to this point.

I was just eighteen and had my whole life in front of me. It was hard to view it positively in the light of my grim situation. Here was a man, quite uninspiring and unattractive, but he was presenting to me the possibility of hope.

Rebekkah Clark

I must have stayed long enough for the Holy Spirit to bring conviction my way, such that I felt I should give this 'Jesus' a try. (That was somewhat difficult, as I was looking for a tangible presence, and there *was* none.) I was invited into a mobile vehicle unit from which someone was preaching, with others talking outside to people in the street. I didn't want to go into the vehicle with someone I didn't even know, so I bravely (or stubbornly) said, 'what's wrong with me giving my life to Jesus right here in the street? Surely it doesn't matter *where* I am?' The man must have been somewhat surprised at my request, but I knelt down on the pavement and was asked to pray 'the sinners prayer.'

The man explained that I might not necessarily feel anything different at all, but that by faith, at my invitation, Jesus would come into my life. I prayed, and was somehow assured that the Lord Jesus knew me as I confessed my sin and received His forgiveness. I committed my life to Him and it felt as though He was pouring oil in me, from the top of my head to the tips of my toes and fingers. I felt the same sensation on the outside, on my head and body, and it was warm, cleansing and comforting.

I did not know a word of the Bible at that time, but this is described in there as the oil of gladness. I was so filled with the Holy Spirit and the love of Jesus that I felt overwhelming joy and love. It was as though a huge burden had been lifted from my shoulders and I simply wanted to hug everyone in sight!

Now the desire to *live* was stronger than I had ever known. For the first time, I had something, no, Someone to live for, a real purpose for my life. I came to realise too, that feelings and insights can be very wrong. I *was* loved, but could not see this because of all the difficulties surrounding and perhaps masking, that love.

Little did I know that God had planned my future for me and that it was all settled even before the world was created. God's Word says so.

I found myself in a vibrant Christian youth group through which I met my husband and together we have sought to put the Lord first in everything. While my husband developed the more conventional ministry of leading and preaching, as the years went by, I found myself more and more involved personally with individuals and this book gives just an insight into this ministry.

Please note that there is a Prayer at the end of this book for you to say if you too would like to receive forgiveness for your sins, and to commit your life to Jesus and experience His great love for you. You can do it right now, or when you have finished the book and seen how wonderful Jesus is. If you pray this Prayer I would love to hear from you so please contact me on rebekkahclark@btinternet.com

Rebekkah Clark

I SURRENDER ALL

'Take your son, your only son – yes, Isaac, whom you love so much – and go to the land of Moriah. Sacrifice him there as a burnt offering on one of the mountains, which I will point out to you.' (Genesis 22 v 2)

"Will you give up everything for *me*?" I heard God ask me. Without hesitation I answered, "Yes of course Lord, I surrender all," feeling rather pleased with myself at the ease with which I could respond.

The following day we had an outreach barbeque in our garden, to which a great number of people came. It got rather cold and what seemed like a great army moved into the house. We had a lovely time with some wonderful fellowship, the evening ending with praise to the Lord.

The next morning my husband and I just thanked the Lord richly for the many blessings and victories that had taken place the previous evening. I had great joy in my heart, singing praises as I tackled the carpet, which needed food and stains to be removed. I was still on my knees when I reached the piano. I noticed, to my horror, that large chips of wood had been gouged out. I started to weep at the thought of the damage done to 'My lovely piano.' "Oh Lord, not *my* piano," I heard in my spirit. "You didn't surrender that possession to *me*, did you?"

Suddenly, the doorbell rang. I jumped up, making some attempt to dry my tears and tidy my appearance. I opened the door. Standing there was a leading Bible teacher who lived a distance away, a very dear friend of ours. He was on his way to speak at a meeting in London, but the Holy Spirit had directed him to drive to our house and ask me if he could have, '*My* piano.' I told him he could now, but it would have been a very different situation a few minutes earlier. Our friend didn't want it of course, and went on his way. One more step of obedience taken, but there were more to follow.

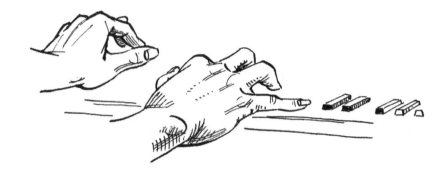

The next morning I heard God say, "Today I require you to surrender your husband and children." I tried to reason with Him, not knowing what to do and in which order. He replied, "Give them to Me in the order that I gave them to you." I struggled as I remembered the story of Abraham being asked to sacrifice his son Isaac in Genesis 22. However God had provided a ram at the last minute and Isaac was saved. I needed reassurance that my husband and children would be spared after I obeyed.

I felt I should attend a midweek communion service held at a local church. I sat on my own at the back as this battle raged within me. The service started and it would soon be my turn to take my place at the communion rail. I still saw in my mind Abraham offering up Isaac on the altar. I finally made a decision to be obedient and found peace returning to me. God is sovereign and His ways are higher than mine. I may not always understand them, but I need to trust them. I went forward to the altar, remembering thankfully the sacrifice that Jesus had made for me in laying down *His* life. I felt tears streaming down my face as I prepared to receive the bread and wine.

Just then a voice spoke, "The Lord is pleased with the sacrifice you have just laid on the altar." The man knew nothing of my struggle, but God had used him. I was learning not to lean on my own understanding, or to the desires or gratification of the flesh. Painful though it was, it was more important for me to be obedient, because my desire was to walk in the Spirit and trust God in everything.

Over the years, I've been tempted many times to go back on my promise, but the experience was too painful to have to repeat. Those sacrifices took me a step further in my walk with God... 'From one degree of glory to another.'

WHEN BILLY GRAHAM
CAME TO TOWN

'Jesus told him, "I am the Way, the Truth and the Life. No one can come to the Father except through me."' (John 14 v 6)

Do you remember Billy Graham and those wonderful evangelistic crusades? How they seemed to change even the surrounding atmosphere for good. How they brought people together and how even the railway stations, trains, buses and streets were filled with the singing of hymns and praise songs. Wonderful times. Wonderful opportunities. Wonderful memories.

I recall one particular time when Billy Graham came to London. These were such good opportunities for the gospel to be heard. I took full advantage of that by asking my Non-Christian friends if they would like to come and sing in a choir in front of a large crowd, such as, for example, the story in 'Give What I Tell You' in Chapter 3. (Well, even the apostle Paul said he used 'all means' to win the lost!)

Another time I managed to get two tickets to Earls Court 'for an evening out' for my mother and her friend (who lived in London) because I really longed for her to believe in God and become a Christian and I prayed that God would do the rest.

When I arrived for the practice and took my place in the choir, the atmosphere was charged with expectancy, curiosity and anticipation. As we started to practise, my heart sent up prayers that my mother and her friend would come and respond to the powerful message of the gospel – that God so loved the world that He sent His only Son, that whoever *believes* in Him will not perish but have everlasting life. Please Lord; let them hear with their hearts. Let them believe.

Choir practice over, we sat down, watching the auditorium gradually fill. We heard that the overflow rooms were also at capacity. Marvellous! Gazing around I suddenly saw two familiar figures making their way to the front. Yes, you've guessed – my mother and her friend! No Lord! The front three rows were cordoned off for the Crusade counsellors, and I cringed as I watched. With total disregard for the barriers, my mother moved them and the two sat down in the very front row! I could see them rejoicing at their good fortune at finding those two empty seats. I kept quiet as I heard other choir members commenting on their antics!

Majestic music signalled the start of the meeting and the choir rose to sing with gusto such wonderful gospel hymns as *And Can It Be, How Great Thou Art, Blessed Assurance, All To Jesus I Surrender* and Beverley Shea sang very movingly *Were You There When They Crucified My Lord?*

Then Billy Graham rose and took his stand at the podium. He preached the simple yet powerful message of God's Gospel of Love – God loved, God gave His Son Jesus, Jesus died, was raised to life again having taken our sin upon Himself, so that we might be brought back into relationship with God.

It was a poignant moment as the invitation was given for those present to accept God's free offer of salvation through the shed blood of the Lord Jesus Christ.

The congregation sang, 'Just as I am without one plea, but that Thy blood was shed for me' - even some of us in the choir had tears in our eyes as we witnessed crowds coming forward in response. My eyes scanned the front seats, my view somewhat blocked by the many people standing there. The seats were all empty as the counsellors had moved to officiate. All empty! My heart leapt excitedly as I believed that my mother and her friend must have stepped forward for salvation. I started to pass on the good news to my friends in the choir who were thrilled for me.

The crowds were slowly moved off to the counselling rooms – and then my heart sank with disappointment. There was my mother and her friend still calmly sitting completely on their own, in the front row - chatting!

I am so happy though, to be able to report that she *did* eventually understand fully the gospel of salvation and later asked Jesus to come into her life at a Full Gospel Business Men's dinner.

REACHING OUT

'Draw close to God, and God will draw close to you.' (James 4 v 8a)

One of my joys was when my family would meet together at the swimming baths with all the grandchildren. The youngest, at the time, was about six months old and just mastering the dog paddle. We'd be there with him in the water, and that gave him confidence.

On one occasion I moved a step or two away from him, just enough to encourage him to swim towards me. I never took my eyes away from him for a second. Some of the time he was on top of the water, but at other times the effort seemingly would cause him to sink, gasping and spluttering wildly. I would stretch out my hands and he kept coming. Over the weeks he accomplished more and more until he was able to swim. We were all very thrilled and proud.

With this picture in mind the Lord asked me a question. "Who actually achieved that, you or your grandson?" I pondered. Both of us needed each other and yet it was actually my little grandson who'd accomplished the feat.

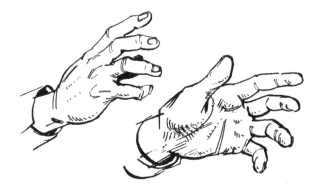

It was as though the Lord smiled and showed me that He too employs similar methods in His initial training of us. In the beginning we know He is there right alongside us, encouraging and enabling. As we grow, He takes a step back, encouraging us forward and onward to a deeper faith walk with Himself.

Of course He never leaves us nor forsakes us. That's His promise. He is with us wherever we go, but His methods stretch and motivate, and we are matured as our trust and confidence increases in Him.

He is instrumental in working His life *in* us, and then He instructs us to work *out* that godliness.

We co-operate with God – and discover that there are no limits to what we can achieve.

Rebekkah Clark

THIS IS CHURCH FOLKS

"You cannot be my disciple if you do not carry your own cross and follow me." (Luke 14 v 27)

Our church leaders had a request for my husband and I. Would we please lead a House group? Of course we would!

We had absolutely no idea what we had let ourselves in for! Very soon we had a House group, mostly containing ex-convicts, former drug addicts, reformed alcoholics and other very troubled people! The leaders later explained that they and others could not take this group on, but they had every confidence in us! We saw it as a challenge that we would have to rise to.

Eventually, most of them were to become Christians and on two occasions, my husband even wrote character reference letters to judges to help get reprieves from prison sentences!

On one occasion, in the very early days, Christmas was approaching and I suggested we go out onto the streets to sing carols.

As people would be at home watching television and might not hear us, I thought that we would be of more use if some of us knocked on doors and asked if anyone in the house had a need that they'd like us to pray for. (It never dawned on me that the appearance of some in the group might be a bit daunting.) Everyone readily agreed to this idea and it was a very rewarding evening. Just how much was unveiled when we returned to the house for our Bible study.

One of the ex-convicts (not yet a Christian) stated, "I have collected a nice sum of money." Expecting that others would have too, he calmly emptied his pockets and smugly handed over the contents! He didn't know it was not our intention to collect money but simply to pray for people

We must never underestimate people in their raw state because God can make remarkable changes in their lives. Some of these people are now leaders, in ministries of their own, working for the Kingdom of God.

The ex-convict who 'collected' the money has since been converted, been through Bible College and now has a prison ministry telling inmates of his own story and that Jesus can completely change their lives too.

THE LOVER OF MY SOUL

'As the Father has loved me, so have I loved you. Now remain in my love.' (John 15 v 9 NIV)

I was lying in bed one night feeling so bereft of God's love. The reality was that I was very loved. I was looking for affirmation and acceptance, thinking that I was of no use to anybody and not understanding my real purpose for being alive. The devil is a liar!

I suddenly felt a hand taking mine. I should have been petrified yet I somehow knew this was the hand of the Lord – I didn't open my eyes to have a look in case He withdrew. I felt such a peace and a sense of awe in the room. The hand brushed my forehead in comfort, as one would a child's. I was very conscious that I was being calmed. My feet were aching and then I felt His hands massaging them. I was reminded that Jesus answers even before we ask.

I remember talking to the Lord and asking Him why it was I didn't 'feel' loved when I knew all the time that He loved me dearly and I was even now experiencing the tangible out-workings of that love. I heard Him reply in my spirit, "I will show you how much I do love you." The most amazing thing happened next and the only way I can humanly explain it is to say that I came out of my body and was looking down at myself lying on the bed.

There were no video cameras in those days and I could *never* have been able to view this scene in the way that God was now showing me. Here I was, front, side, back – oh, and the Lord seemed to take me *inside* myself and He showed me my heart and the love that was in it.

He showed me inside my mind and how my thoughts were directed towards Him. He was showing me how *He* viewed me, not as I viewed myself. This was *so* important as it now didn't seem to matter *what* others thought about me, or indeed, what *I* thought about myself. Jesus thought I was beautiful inside and out and was showing me how *He* enjoys looking at me, hearing from me and being with me.

Because of that beautiful experience, I remembered what had happened when I gave my life to Jesus. I became His servant and His love had been deposited in my heart so that in due season, it could overflow to others.

That experience changed my life and subsequently prepared me for the problems that I was going to encounter in the ministry He has given me. I know now who I am in Christ and this is more important to me than anything else in life and it cannot be taken from me.

CHILDLIKE FAITH

'He (Jesus) said to them, "Let the children come to me. Don't stop them! For the Kingdom of God belongs to such as these. I assure you, anyone who doesn't have their kind of faith will never get into the Kingdom of God."' (Mark 10 v 14b,15)

A convoy of cars took off from the manse, heading for a gospel crusade in town. The same convoy later returned. As we walked into the manse there was a wonderful aroma wafting from the kitchen, that of a roast dinner. It smelt really inviting.

It had been a long morning and I glanced across at my three small children. I could see their mouths watering but how was I going to tell them that we hadn't anything so delicious to eat?

As we journeyed home it was a relief that the children didn't ask if we too had a roast meal awaiting us, because times had been hard. Instead, one of the children suddenly said, "I'd love an egg for my lunch."

I was still smelling the roast! When another voice chimed in "I'd like some bread to go with it so that we can have egg on toast." At which the third cried out, " I'd like some orange squash!" I gently chided her by commenting that it was perhaps a little extravagant to ask the Lord for orange squash and that water would be more than sufficient. Their childlike faith was not about to be deterred however and they had no qualms about asking the Lord to provide these items for their lunch. It had become an exciting game.

We pulled up at home and the children could hardly wait to get out of the car. They just about stayed until I had checked that it was safe and gave permission. They raced up the steps and to the front door, their expectancy high. Their prayers had been answered! There on the doorstep were a dozen eggs, a loaf of bread and yes – a bottle of orange squash. Childlike faith had been amply rewarded.

These were lessons in trusting God. Another time the children had set the table and we had all sat down to give thanks for the meal. As we finished praying, the doorbell rang and a neighbour stood there holding a tray of hot tureens. "Could you use these, as my guests have cancelled?" Her dinner was already prepared and ready for the eating. We gratefully sat down and relished this feast of delights as her meal was more nutritious than mine.

God doesn't always work in the same way but He is always so faithful, especially in our times of greatest need. Sometimes we were given food or money in advance. Living by faith required that we never mentioned our lack to others. We marvelled at God's grace as He prompted others to be obedient.

So much of the time in the past we had been the givers, but for now, God was teaching others to do that, and we were having to learn how to receive. It reminded me that God used even ravens to bring food to Elijah. Although we were out of control, God never was and gave to us time and time again out of His plentiful storehouse.

GOD IS INTERESTED IN EVEN THE SIMPLE THINGS

'We can be confident that He will listen to us whenever we ask Him for anything in line with His will.' (1 John 5 v 14)

My husband's faith walk with the Lord concerns the more practical things in life. He started asking the Lord which checkout we should use in our local supermarket and he was encouraged when a number came into his thoughts and he would discover that either there was a very short queue or perhaps that a checkout had just been opened up.

On one occasion, when in a great hurry, there were long queues at every checkout, except the one in the middle, to which the Lord had directed him, which had no queue at all. Had the Lord made the checkout invisible to those waiting to pay?

When we were in need of a certain household item my husband would pray and ask the Lord where to go for the best deal, or which shop would have what we were looking for. There was the occasion when we were in need of a coffee table and the name of a shop came to him, so off we went. The only problem was that when we arrived, the shop did not sell furniture! It turned out, however that the shop next door did and had an ideal coffee table in the window. It was just what we were looking for and at a greatly reduced price.

My husband wasn't deterred when he found he was one shop out and finds that, for some reason, this still is often the case. He thus recognizes that the Lord is sovereign and uses what faith we have and increases such faith as we step out.

Chapter 2

LIFE ABUNDANT

Learn to interpret correctly

That's my God

In your dreams

Pregnant pause

A notion about a potion

Conference supplies

Just pray

A murder averted

LEARN TO INTERPRET CORRECTLY

'Let me tell about the visions and revelations I received from the Lord.' (2 Corinthians 12 v 1b)

I once had a picture (or 'vision') in my mind, given to me by God. It was the first time such a thing had happened and I mustered up the faith to speak out what I saw.

We had recently enjoyed the experience of 'the Baptism of the Holy Spirit' and were meeting with other Christians keen to learn more. The church to which we then belonged would not accept us once we had this Spirit-filled life or allow us to express ourselves through the Gifts of the Spirit. We therefore met in one another's homes to pray and learn more from the Word of God about this new experience. It had happened to five families, all within a space of just eight days, and in three different venues! Two families on a Sunday, ourselves midweek and two more families in another church the following Sunday. God was on the move!

Back to my 'vision', it was of a coffin covered with a Union Jack and placed at the verycentre of the church. After I had shared it with the group, a woman at the meeting believed she knew 'who was in that coffin.' She gave the name of a church elder whom I loved dearly. I was shocked, because I thought he was going to die.

After the service on the following Sunday I was speaking to this elder, who was losing the sight in his eyes. I asked him, "Would you rather have your sight restored, or have a deeper experience of Jesus?" Of course he immediately chose the latter which made me wonder if the interpretation was correct.

I still didn't have further light on what I saw in the picture, but meditated on it for a long time. Someone invited us to a House Fellowship where we knew most of the leaders and people who attended. The praise and worship was wonderful, and afterwards,

I was keen to question our leader friend about the vision and the understanding of it. As I told him, I started to cry, as I did not want that dear elder to die. My leader friend had great wisdom and maturity in God and said that the vision was all right, but the interpretation that we had was incorrect.

Our leader friend explained that like the interpretation of parables, vision interpretations are always simple. Then he went on to give what he believed was the correct meaning of the vision. "This man is not going to die but he is going to be the death of that church." Although he was a very keen Christian, he resisted the things of the Spirit and led others accordingly. He did ultimately die many years later, but not before the death of the church. Sadly, what had been a flourishing, well-attended House of God, because of his resistance was reduced to a few members in a short space of time.

This was our first time of learning about interpretation. My husband and I both found it very helpful as we recognised how differently things can be viewed. We realized that everything must come from the Holy Spirit.

It was a learning curve, and I could have missed what God was *really* saying.

THAT'S MY GOD

' And I command you before God, who gives life to all ...' (1 Timothy 6 v 13a)

I heard the chug of a diesel taxi as it pulled up next door. Looking out of the window I saw my heavily pregnant neighbour arriving home. She was about eight months at the time.

I sensed in my spirit that something was not right and hurried next door. I peeked through her window and saw her sobbing uncontrollably. I tapped, motioning for her to let me in, which she did. She then slumped to the floor and I sat there with her, hugging her and praying some comfort back into her desolate form. I waited for the tears to subside and once calmer, she began to share her grief.

She had been to the hospital for a normal pre-natal check-up, only to be told by the doctors that the baby she was carrying was dead! It would arrive in due time – stillborn!

The Spirit of God rose up within me and I cried out to my Creator God. "Put life and breath back into this baby's body – in Jesus'

Name!" As I prayed, I laid hands on the mother's womb and the baby suddenly leapt back into life!

Within a month, my neighbour gave birth to a beautiful, perfect and healthy baby boy.

That's my God!

IN YOUR DREAMS

'If I had the gift of prophecy, and if I knew all the mysteries of the future and knew everything about everything, but didn't love others, what good would I be?' (1 Corinthians 13 v 2a)

My neighbour's husband had a job that was to take him out of the country and they therefore all moved abroad. Whilst back here on business, he came to visit and have a meal with us. He did not believe in God and often used to scoff or mock should the conversation move on to Christian topics. He once joked, "Allow *me* to pack your case for you if you think you might be taken up in the rapture." (The rapture is a future event when all born again Christians are taken up to heaven.)

Then, together with them (those who have gone before), we who are still alive and remain on the earth will be caught up in the clouds to meet the Lord in the air and remain with Him forever.'
(1 Thessalonians 4 v 17).

It so happened that I'd had a prophetic dream the previous evening, concerning his wife. I plucked up the courage to share it with him. I saw, in my dream, that she was back home in England. She had with her their two children. Her husband was of course away. She came to tell me that the shower had broken. She was pregnant and found it difficult to wash her long hair without a shower. I offered her the use of my own. She had coffee afterwards and she then went back home.

My dream continued with the phone ringing in the early hours of the morning. It was my neighbour asking if we could take her to the hospital. She was having contractions although only in her seventh month. My husband kindly obliged and I took charge of her two children.

Still in my dream we all went to visit her later that day, to see the newborn addition. It was a little girl, weighing just five pounds. Her premature birth meant that she was now in an incubator. Mother was doing well and I asked her what she was going to call her daughter. She wanted to name her after one of my own children, so I suggested she might add her own middle name as well.

My dream ended with the family visiting England once again. Their daughter was now four years old, with long dark hair reaching down her back.

When I had finished telling the husband about the dream he scoffed remarking, "My wife is not pregnant nor likely to be. Furthermore, she is visiting relatives abroad."

He later told us that his wife had called him that very evening to say that she had seen a doctor, as she had been feeling unwell. His diagnosis was, "You are pregnant!" As she was living in a primitive country, it was suggested that it would be better for her to come to England to have the baby.

Everything that I had seen in my dream came to pass in every detail. Even my neighbour's husband had to agree that it was remarkable.

PREGNANT PAUSE

'The fruit of your womb will be blessed.' (Deuteronomy 28 v 4a NIV)

A young Christian couple with a baby boy moved into the house next door. About this time I had another prophetic dream. This dream showed the woman becoming pregnant with a baby girl. After what happened in the last story, I thought I would perhaps keep this to myself. However, the Holy Spirit told me, "She will come to see you today, and I want you to give her the good news." I struggled over this. After all, pregnancy is a personal matter and something which she may well like to discover for herself. On the other hand, it could be confirmation for her.

Whilst sitting in my garden enjoying a cup of tea, my new neighbour came round. She looked very unhappy. I shared with her the content of my dream and, to my surprise, she perked up and was really blessed. She had been asking the Lord for another child! The Holy Spirit said to me, "Tell her she is *already* pregnant!" I did so and suggested she went for a test. It proved positive!

I realized then that I might have a God-given anointing to pray for babies. When another couple later came to us for counselling, I could see they clearly longed for a family. They so far had been unable to conceive. I laid hands on the wife's womb and prayed for fruitfulness. I told them, "It needs 'faith and works.' You *will* be fruitful, now go and play your part!"

The girl maintains she became pregnant that very night, for just nine months later, she gave birth to a beautiful baby girl. Three subsequent children followed!

A NOTION ABOUT A POTION

'I tell you this: Whatever you prohibit on earth is prohibited in heaven, and whatever you allow on earth is allowed in heaven.'
(Matthew 18 v 18)

My husband and I were invited to visit some very good friends that we hadn't seen for a long while. We arrived to find a problem with their son who was upstairs in bed. I asked if there was anything I could do.

The wife reminded me that her son had suffered from asthma from the time he was a baby. Today he was having a very serious attack and she felt that she should not leave him for a minute. I offered to pray with him but was told that he wouldn't let anyone near him and kept fighting people away. However she asked me to pray from downstairs.

We gathered together and started to pray, and I had a picture of a black plastic dustbin bag full of clothes. Further I 'saw' a book in the bottom of the bag and also some sort of medication, or potion. I knew in my spirit that evil was connected with the book and it turned out that it was about spiritualism and incantations.

I felt very strange asking my friend if she knew anything about the black bag, but her answer was reassuring as she immediately responded, "Yes, one arrived today from a neighbour across the road." Her neighbour, who was a spiritualist, had given her some second-hand clothes for her children. I mentioned the book and the potion. "Oh! I gave him some of the liquid which I believed to be medicine to help him."

As my friend reflected on what had happened, she realised that it was about that time that her son's asthma had worsened. She hadn't connected his condition with the medicine. The book? She had put it into the bin because as a Christian it was not something that had interested her. I suggested she burn the book, as I believed it had been deliberately given to her. I also asked her to fetch the potion, which I destroyed.

I encouraged her and said we would pray that the Holy Spirit would cleanse her son's system and I also suggested, on a practical basis, that he should drink plenty of water to dilute the effects. We also bound the spirits connected with everything that had been given to my friend by her neighbour. The boy's asthma attack ceased and, even better, as far as I am aware he never had another one.

Praise the Lord! The Holy Spirit versus an evil potion – no contest!

CONFERENCE SUPPLIES

'If you give, you will receive. Your gift will return to you in full measure, pressed down, shaken together to make room for more, and running over. Whatever measure you use in giving - large or small - it will be used to measure what is given back to you.'
(Luke 6 v 38)

My husband and I were at a Christian Conference in Devon. At this particular meeting we were requested to pray and ask the Lord how much He would have us give in the offering. The organisers explained how much the conference costs were and that they were believing that God would prompt each individual and that the full amount would be received.

My husband was the one who usually gave on our behalf after we agreed an amount. I don't know why, but I had a real desire to give to the Lord an offering directly from myself. I rarely handled the money and so didn't have any with me. The Holy Spirit knew my heart and said, "Look in your pockets." I thought therefore that I might have left some loose change in one of them at some time in the past. It happens.

My coat was draped across the chair in front of me. No one had gone near it. I reached for it and to my astonishment; it was weighed down by the fullness of coins in my pocket! I was totally amazed. I somehow thought that the offering might have been multiplied supernaturally or something 'spiritual' like that. Instead, God was just as spectacular but on a much more practical level. I had a figure in mind that I wanted to give and the coins (large denominations) added up to the exact amount!

Postscript – *as we returned to our hotel we met a young couple. They were concerned that they couldn't get home as their car had engine trouble and it just would not start. They had believed the Lord to get them down to Devon and my husband and I assured them we could believe the Lord for their return journey. We laid hands on the car and commanded it to, "Go! In Jesus' Name." – which it did!*

The Lord is interested in every single detail of our lives and wants us to involve Him in them.

JUST PRAY

'Keep on praying.' (1 Thessalonians 5 v17)

I watched from the window as a funeral procession went by. I had a strong desire to pray for the family in the car. I found I did this almost by compulsion, each time I saw a funeral procession. It's a habit I have never broken.

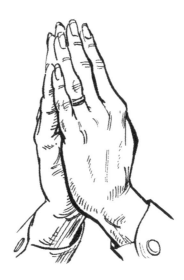

I was out driving one day and halted my car to allow a funeral procession to pass. I didn't feel I should pray for anyone's salvation, but instead asked the Lord for comfort for the family, and that God would enable them to bid their farewells to the deceased.

The next day we received a phone call from a man who was the son of a very close and lovely lady friend of ours whom we loved dearly. He told us that she had died and they had held a close family funeral and it turned out to be the same funeral that I had prayed for. So clearly the Lord had led me to pray for my friend's family at the time they were passing by. It thrilled me to know that I had heard the voice of my Lord and had prayed accordingly.

This made me wonder who prays for me that I don't know about?

A MURDER AVERTED.

'What this means is that those who become Christians become new persons. They are not the same anymore, for the old life is gone. A new life has begun!' (2 Corinthians 5 v 17)

It was a Saturday evening and there was a sudden knock on the door. My husband opened it and we recognised the young girl. "I've someone in the car. He's in a bit of a state and has many problems. I heard about his problems and I believe you can help him. Do you think I could bring him in; I'm not sure what to do?"

She brought him in; he sat down and began to explain that he had had a serious row with someone he knew and now he was on his way to collect a gun to go and kill him. Our young friend had overheard this and was frantically doing everything she could think of to avert the murder. All she could think of was to bring him to our house.

We talked at length with him and explained the gospel message and the truth about Jesus and His great love for us whatever we may have done or wanted to do. The time went on and about four hours later at two in the morning I said to the man, "I'm going to get on my knees. If you want to give your life to Jesus, you do the same."

He fell to his knees (as we all did) and crying tearfully he gave his life to the Lord and then he actually prayed for his estranged wife and the person he had set out to kill. A new man indeed!

We heard later that he had returned to his wife.

No one ever knows what a day will bring!

P.S. A day or two later, when I was out shopping I met the girl again. This time I felt it right to caution her of the danger that she could have put herself into by getting into the man's car to bring him to our house, especially as he was intent on murder. In this case it worked out well but we must always be sensible as the devil is always seeking ways to do us harm.

Chapter 3

GOD CAN SPEAK ANYTIME ANYWHERE

HEARING AND GOING

LOUD AND CLEAR

LEARNING CURVES

MORE BATHTIME MUSINGS

SPEAKING IN SPANISH

DIVINE APPOINTMENTS

SPEAK WHAT I TELL YOU

GIVE WHAT I TELL YOU

HEARING AND GOING

'When they call on me, I will answer.' (Psalm 91 v 15a)

I used to start my morning with a bath rather than a shower (this was my prayer closet). I would use the bath as a visual aid, acting out physically what was happening spiritually. I would run some water into the bath and then remove the plug. As the water disappeared down the plughole I would visualize the enemy going down with it.

Now I could fill the bath and enjoy a relaxing soak while confessing my sin and having my time of worship with the Lord. I would now really feel that I was a clean channel through which the Holy Spirit could speak. Praying in tongues, I would often receive an English interpretation for particular people or situations.

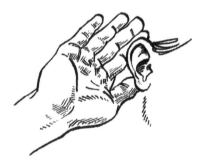

I recalled verses from Psalm 91. 'Those who live in the shelter of the Most High will find rest in the shadow of the Almighty' (v.1) and 'When they call on me, I will answer' (v.15a). I put this into practice and began to receive very clear answers and directives from God. For example, I was to go to a certain house at a specific time. "Knock on the door and only as it is opened will I tell you what to say." Wow! Some test of obedience. Not wanting to be embarrassed, my pride could always allow me to say I'd called at the wrong house.

However, as I was just learning in these faith ventures, the Lord was very gentle and reassuring. These first steps were quite easy. As I grew though, the harder it seemed. The battleground is the mind and I frequently suffered the attack of the enemy. I knew lonely times and had no-one to share with who would understand.

Back to the doorstep. A lady opened the door and simply said, "Can I help you?" Great! I falteringly explained why I'd come to her. Words started to flow from my mouth and I realised that the Lord was speaking profoundly to that woman.

At first her expression was unchanging, but her strong and composed stance suddenly crumpled before me as she broke down and sobbed. I waited until her tears subsided. She then shared her situation.

I eventually left her – myself humbled and awestruck by a powerful and all-knowing God. It was my privilege to be a vessel in His service.

LOUD AND CLEAR

'Then the Lord caused the donkey to speak.' (Numbers 22 v 28a)

This particular morning I was having my daily bathtime worship with the Lord. I enjoyed these intimate moments with God. No one to disturb me or make demands on my time. I used this time to listen for the Lord to speak to me. I knew His voice, usually by that inner witness in the heart. Today though, was enough to blow my mind!

The devil had been playing havoc with my thoughts, attempting to convince and persuade me that I was not conscious of the Lord's leading. It was all a ploy to destroy my faith in God. The Lord had spoken to me and assured me that it was Him. To my natural logic this seemed not only unreasonable, but altogether absurd. "Is this really *You*?" I pleaded.

I gasped because the answer came back to me loud and clear. I do mean that. Absolutely audibly – and just so there was no mistake – the voice came – through the taps! The Lord confirmed what He had given me to do, and reassured me. Wow!

If God can record in His Word that He spoke through a donkey – who am I to doubt that He can confront my questionings through a tap!

Rebekkah Clark

LEARNING CURVES

'Then the Lord spoke to Jonah a second time: "Get up and go to the great city of Nineveh, and deliver the message of judgement I have given you."' (Jonah 3 v 1,2)

A bath a day keeps the housework away! Well at least on the other side of the door for a while. Another splash session and I heard the Lord speaking in my spirit, "Go to this particular village and to a certain house there." I immediately recognised the place as belonging to a lady I knew. My response? I ignored the instruction. I had 'my plans'.

To be honest, I had been having some problems with that old enemy – DOUBT. Remember the Garden of Eden – "Has God *said*?" In my spirit I saw the lady I knew, broken-hearted with head in hands. She was weeping – sobbing would be a more apt assessment.

I didn't know if this was 'for real' and so continued to dress and get ready to go out. The name of the village kept tumbling around in my thoughts, but I pushed this aside as 'coincidence' and kept my coffee date with a friend.

All the same, I felt very uncomfortable in my spirit the whole time I was there. I excused myself and went to the bathroom. The Lord sometimes spoke to me there. I can't imagine why (!), but I distinctly felt the Lord's disapproval. Moreover, I *knew* I should have gone to the lady in the other village! "All *right* Lord! I'm still *learning!*" I mentioned this to my friend and she agreed that I should go.

Don't you just know it? I got into the car – and it wouldn't start! I prayed and it eventually spluttered into motion, but would only operate in first gear. It just sort of bucked the whole journey at a very slow pace. (What did you say? Wouldn't have happened if I'd obeyed in the first place!) I can tell you it was a most uncomfortable experience inside *and* out, and the distance not a short one! I knew it was an 'enemy attack' trying to prevent me from getting to a very important appointment.

After what seemed like hours I arrived at the very sweet village cottage and knocked on the door, myself now in need of the Balm of Gilead on certain anatomical areas! "Hallo, how are you?" I mouthed as cheerily as I could muster. The lady looked perfectly all right in *my* opinion. Nevertheless I said, "The Lord directed me here." She then invited me in - for coffee. (I know. I needn't have gone and had that first cup!)

I started to speak as the Holy Spirit gave me the words and I explained that I had 'seen' her very troubled and disturbed with her head in her hands. "That's right," she mumbled. "It was earlier today." She mentioned the time (you've guessed) but she felt that the Lord had ignored and forsaken her. He *had* tried to send *me*. I was reminded of Jonah who, like me, did not go the first time and also of Isaiah when God said to him, "Whom shall I send?" but he replied, "Here am I, send me."

The lady shared a deep problem and we were able to pray it through together. I was also able to pray for the baptism of the Holy Spirit for her, which she received and began to speak in tongues, dancing joyfully around her room.

The telephone rang. Her husband had been taking lunch on his work's roof garden when his back suddenly 'went.' He couldn't move and was in severe pain. I prayed with him over the phone and his back eased a little. I invited him to call round to my house in the evening, when I knew my husband would be home, if he were in further need of help. I thought no more of it as I knew he was a little sceptical about these things. However, he arrived, doubled up with the pain.

My children were occupying most of the rooms doing homework. I knew my husband was due home at any moment and so I took the man to the only other free room to pray. (I realised with hindsight that it is *not* wisdom to minister to a member of the opposite sex alone. I emphasize this most strongly).

First I prayed for the protection of the blood of Jesus over my household. Then I asked the man to kneel down. I also knelt and asked him to be quiet whilst I waited on the Lord for guidance. He became irritated at the length of the silence but I was not prepared to minister in my own strength. His agitation grew but then I shared with him the word of knowledge that I'd been waiting for God to give to me. His arrogant and rebellious stance changed immediately and tears filled his eyes.

His problem was unforgiveness. But soon he repented and forgave the person. I then declared, "In Jesus' Name you are now healed. Get up and walk!" He lost patience at this point and dismissed the proceedings as nonsense. What he did not realise however, was that he was being healed because he stormed out of the house!

As the man went home his physical healing was in progress, but he was also in need of further soul healing. He grumpily announced to his wife that he was going to bed and then *ran* up the stairs! He still seemed oblivious to his healing, and when his wife came to bed, he told her that he did not want to go to hospital for an operation, having an aversion to hospitals. "You're healed," his wife proclaimed. "I saw you *run* upstairs!" However, her husband was still struggling to come to terms with what was actually going on!

During the night, his wife awoke to find the bed soaking wet and her husband's pyjamas saturated. This was the Holy Spirit completing the healing work of body, mind and spirit. The Lord had performed His very own operation on the man – while he slept!

He never did have to go into that hospital. Praise the Lord!

MORE BATHTIME MUSINGS

'For if I pray in tongues, my spirit is praying, but I don't understand what I am saying. Well then, what shall I do? I will do both. I will pray in the spirit, and I will pray in words I understand.'
(1 Corinthians 14 v 14,15)

I remember another bathtime encounter, this time demonstrating how the Holy Spirit intercedes for and with us as we allow Him. As I was relaxing I prayed for various topics as they came to me. The name of someone very dear to me kept interrupting the flow of my thoughts and the Lord was telling me that she was dying. I shrugged this off as a mistake and continued with 'my praying,' using my prayer language.

God was insistent however, and her name kept coming to mind together with the same information. At last I believed it to be the Lord speaking. I began to pray earnestly until I felt the burden lift.

Some months later I was travelling with the person and unexpectedly learnt what had taken place. She had been battling a situation with God and resisting Him with all her might. The end result was that she was taken seriously ill with pneumonia. She had literally been at the point of death when she yielded to the Lord and her healing was instantaneous. I discovered that this incident occurred at the exact date and time of my bathtime prayer session. The Holy Spirit had used my availability as a channel of His deliverance.

How important it is that we keep tuned in to His Presence and promptings. It is sometimes a matter of life or death.

SPEAKING IN SPANISH

'Look! Here I stand at the door and knock. If you hear me calling and open the door, I will come in, and we will share a meal as friends.' (Revelation 3 v 20)

We English abroad are sometimes an amusing sight to behold are we not? Gesticulating wildly, arms flailing everywhere, fingers pointing – all in an effort to make ourselves understood and overcome the obvious lack of local language knowledge.

However, I felt much comforted when on one particular occasion, my new South American neighbour's little boy appeared at my door doing much the same thing. He could hardly speak any English. (Okay – so he *was* only three at the time!) I managed to make out from his little gestures that they had neither oven nor heating working.

I went round to see my neighbour and took with me a camping cooker and portable heater, much to her delight. She was taking English lessons but, as she had only just started these, we had to muddle along as best we could.

Sometime later, I was praying for my neighbour in one of my morning 'bathtime sessions.' I prayed in both my natural and spirit tongue for her. I said to the Lord, 'If you have to change my tongue to her language for me to communicate with her, then please do it!' I then found myself repeating just three words in the pure Spanish tongue as I was later to find out. The Spanish language is much more expressive and explicit than our English one. In my spirit I sensed that these three words conveyed something of the majesty, splendour and holiness of God, indeed somehow even more than that.

God was directing me to go to her house and have coffee with her, which I did.

The text of Revelation 3 v 20, "I stand at the door and knock" sprang to mind as did Holman Hunt's painting of Jesus doing just that. In that picture, the only handle was on the inside of the door. So, there I was standing at the other side of my neighbour's door, knocking and trying to enact what I'd seen and make her understand! She eyed me suspiciously, perhaps wondering if I'd taken leave of my senses.

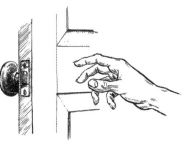

Just then the Holy Spirit interrupted me. "Finished? Why don't you just speak to her the three words that I gave you?" Strange how at times we fail to do even the simplest of tasks God gives to us, isn't it? Could it be that thing called P-R-I-D-E? Okay, Lord, here goes. Nervously I looked straight at her and asked, "Does this word mean anything to you? ...." She was absolutely captivated. Encouraged by this I was spurred on to give her the other two words at which she dropped to her knees, sobbing and then I was prompted by the Holy Spirit to speak further in my new tongue. The Lord had spoken directly to her in her own language. How gracious He is. My previous struggling in the flesh had achieved nothing.

I know we all like happy endings and I'm pleased to report that this dear lady later became a Christian and was filled with the Holy Spirit. She received the gift of tongues and spoke – in perfect English!

DIVINE APPOINTMENTS

'And if you give even a cup of cold water to one of the least of my followers, you will surely be rewarded.' (Matthew 10 v 42)

Nothing happens by chance. One day I looked out of my lounge window and noticed someone walking past. I believe God wanted me to see that person so that I would pray for her. She was a very well dressed woman but she was very distressed and extremely tearful so I felt I should go out to her. Her husband had just died and she felt all alone and didn't know what to do with herself. I was easily able to become God's arms of love, comfort and encouragement for her.

After this I began to take 'divine appointments' very seriously. If I met anyone in the supermarket, or wherever, I believed they were appointments set up by the Lord.

It so happened that an elderly lady literally bumped into me in the Supermarket one day. I thought to myself, "she's just bumped into Jesus and she doesn't know it!" I wanted to bump into everyone after that! I sauntered to the meat counter, and noticed the same elderly lady standing there. She was eyeing a very tiny piece of stuffed, rolled, neck of lamb and fumbling in her purse to see if she had enough money to pay for it. To me, it looked all gristle and no meat and of little worth and I wished she could afford something better. I moved away to do my own shopping.

Well, it so happened that I ended up at the same checkout, behind her. Her shopping was being passed through the scanner. As she was putting it in her bag, the Holy Spirit prompted me very strongly – "I want you to give her the piece of meat *you* bought, *and* pay for her whole shopping bill." The dear woman was still packing away her shopping and was unaware that I had indicated to the cashier what I wanted to do. The elderly lady went to pay and was overwhelmed when she learned that the bill had been settled and she asked me why I would want to do such a thing.

At that moment, I felt the Holy Spirit speaking further. "It's her birthday today and she doesn't have living relatives." She cried when I told her what I knew. She said that no one else knew it was her birthday and, with the cashier listening, I was able to tell her that the most important thing was that *God* knew and He wanted to make it a special day for her.

The Bible says that 'some sow and others reap' and we never know what our loving deeds will produce. One day we'll meet in heaven many of the people whom we have helped in one way or another and who have come to the Lord through the chain, of which we were a link.

SPEAK WHAT I TELL YOU

'To one person the Spirit gives the ability to give wise advice, to another He gives the gift of special knowledge.'
(1 Corinthians 12 v 8)

There was a season in my life when I occasionally went to speak at a number of women's groups. As much as I would try to prepare a message or a song I found that the Lord usually gave me only one word (eg *love*) or a line of a song, or a thought that would apply to wherever I was going. However this one word was always enough to reassure me that the Lord had something that He wanted me to share and that, when the time came, He would give me more. It was obvious to me that the Lord wanted to stretch my faith to trust Him more and more.

I remember on one occasion when I was on the platform, seated and poised in anticipation for what God wanted to do but at that moment I had not received anything at all from God. There were many women gathered for the meeting and the lady introducing me announced that I would be speaking on the subject of ...? She turned and peered at me over her glasses with a smile and an expectant nod of her head, hands cupped, gesturing at me to indicate my topic. I raised my hands, shrugging my shoulders, enough to show her that I did not have a clue.

She tried again, this time declaring that I would be singing, and of course, she wanted to know *what.* I had no idea, although I *did* realise that these people were used to having everything ordered and predictable. Not having a knowledge of the subject or what to sing was a new experience for them as it was for me.

In this case the Lord did not indicate in any way what I was to sing or say until I actually stood up and opened my mouth. It stretched my faith like elastic. I greeted the women present and after singing and giving a short word, the Holy Spirit guided me to go down from the platform and walk behind each row of ladies and speak privately in their ears what He told me to say.

To the first lady I had to say, "The Lord says that the affair you are having with the minister is to stop right now!" To each lady I had to say something personal. It was an incredible time and lives were changed that day, as was the church thereafter.

Never expect God to do things the same way twice. He is a creative God and always ready to work in a different way!

GIVE WHAT I TELL YOU

'So you see, it isn't enough just to have faith. Faith that doesn't show itself by good deeds is no faith at all – it is dead and useless.' (James 2 v 17)

I opened the door. "Hallo" smiled the woman, "would you like to make a contribution to the National Children's Home?" She pushed the tin forward hopefully. My husband and I usually give money as directed by God but I felt I should pop a small donation in the box as it was a worthwhile cause.

She looked at me, smiling broadly. The Holy Spirit prompted me to give whatever money was in the pocket of my coat, hanging up just to the right of me. I boldly ventured, "God has just told me to give you whatever is in my pocket." I mustered all the faith I could (as I didn't think there was *anything* in there) and dipped my hand into the pocket. I was somewhat amazed and shaken to feel paper. I pulled out what was a large quantity of notes and I don't know who was the more shocked as I handed them over! Her mouth dropped open and so did mine as I mentally considered what I could have spent that money on.

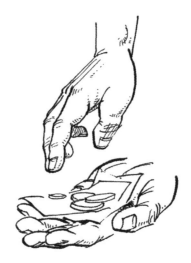

Rebekkah Clark

"This has never happened to me before," she stammered. "Oh," I replied, "That's my God!" At this she mentioned that she lived nearby and had heard singing coming from our open window one day when our House Fellowship had been meeting. She had been watching our lives.

God is so smart. The woman also noticed my hair and mentioned that she was looking for a hairdresser. I told her my daughter had styled it and I offered to make her an appointment, which she accepted.

On the day that she arrived for this appointment, I had just made some homemade soup and I saw her look longingly. "I'll bring some up to you," I offered.

We later got talking and I asked her if she liked singing. "Oh yes," she said enthusiastically. "Would you like to sing in a choir then?" I continued and she jumped at the chance. "Well, your hair's now nicely styled. Would you like to come out tonight and sing?" (There's nothing like striking while the iron's hot!) She gave another positive response and so she became an extra member of the choir at a Luis Pulau Crusade meeting that evening.

She sang and listened to the gospel message and was completely enthralled, asking many questions and talking non-stop in the car on the way home. By the time we arrived at her house, she pleaded with me to pray for her and she gave her life to Jesus right there in the car.

One small act of obedience can pay great dividends.

Chapter 4

MUSICAL INTERLUDE

HONKY TONK ANGEL

SINGING IN THE SPIRIT

HARPING ON ABOUT IT

MUSICAL MIRACLE

WITNESS EVERYWHERE

UNITY PRESERVED

MY CO-WORKER

HONKY TONK ANGEL

'Some Greeks who had come to Jerusalem .... They said,
"Sir we want to meet Jesus."' (John 12 v 20,21)

Not so long ago, two Greek brothers, mature students, were staying with us. We had been talking to them about the Lord whenever they invited us to do so.

One day, they hadn't noticed that my husband and I had had to go out for a short while. On our return we were very surprised to find them outside in the garden on the patio. It was cold and they were shaking – but I saw it was from fear, not from the drop in temperature. I offered to make them a hot drink and although cold, they were adamant that they did not want to step inside the house again. Still trembling, they began to explain.

They had been upstairs in their room when suddenly they heard the most beautiful music being played on the piano. They described it as being somewhere in between classical/heavenly/angelic in sound. They thought I was playing and they listened for a while before creeping out of their room and down the stairs to have a peep. They wanted to make some comment but ...there was nobody at the piano! They immediately rushed back into their bedroom, thinking they had imagined it all.

After a short while, the music started up again and they had another look – nobody was there and in fear they raced outside the house!

Again they heard music and from where they were sitting on the patio they could look through the window and see the piano. They could see the keys moving but no one was playing. This proved to them that the sound wasn't coming from elsewhere and also that they had not imagined it all.

We laughed and explained that clearly angels had paid a visit to our house and such visitors were welcome at any time. They knew of angels from their Catholic upbringing but had never encountered anything like this. Their lives were not right at the time and undoubtedly God was trying to get their attention.

Considerable ministry has taken place in our house over the years but oh the sheer joy of knowing that angels had been playing our piano. What a pity we missed this experience although we have been in meetings where angels have joined in the worship – unforgettable experiences.

Many other people have had similar encounters with angelic beings. One leading man of God describes how a music group were practicing at a church for Sunday worship and had decided to record their efforts – the verse and the chorus. They later played back the recording to discover that the most beautiful angelic choir was singing in harmony with them.

On another occasion, while a service was going on, the music group were playing and the congregation were worshipping, when suddenly, a wonderful chorus of voices joined them. The musicians turned off the amplifiers and stopped playing, but the chorus only grew louder and louder, and in the roof of the church, a huge choir of angels were singing and descending. People were thrown onto the floor, face down and crying out to Jesus in repentance. Others who had left the building were unable to re-enter because of the power of God there.

Some parents tell of their children having seen an angel face to face. Dare we thwart this when God's Word tells us that 'we may entertain angels unawares?'

Unbelievable – no, rather, it's the **super**natural, a dimension every bit as real as the natural to those who have eyes to see and ears to hear.

SINGING IN THE SPIRIT

'Obedience is far better than sacrifice.' (1 Samuel 15 v 22b)

I used to be asked to speak at different churches at women's meetings when I was a young Christian. I didn't really want to do this because I found it extremely hard to study and I would swap from subject to subject, and never know exactly what I was supposed to be speaking about!

Then one day I handed it all over to the Lord. I said, "I can't *do* this. If you want me to do it, You'll need to show me another way that will fit in with my personality." As I waited on the Lord, He spoke to me saying, "Are you prepared to be my mouthpiece and speak what I tell you no matter where you are? This will take faith and trust in a measure you've not known before."

I was very prepared to do this and I found it very exciting to be led by the Holy Spirit and not have to lean on my own understanding. Little did I know just what this was going to mean for my future and the lonely path that I would have to tread.

My first experience of my newfound walk was when my husband (who is a lay preacher) was preaching at a local church. I would always accompany him and sing. We had been doing this for all our married life but on this occasion, I woke up in the morning with no voice and feeling very nauseated. My husband and I agreed that I ought to try and make it to the meeting because we believed it was the devil who didn't want me to be there. I also knew there is healing in the presence of the Lord.

When we arrived at the church I still had no voice. The service started and the time came when my husband would ask me to come forward and sing. He looked at me and I had an overwhelming Holy Spirit desire to go to the front and position myself ready to minister in His ability, which I did. However, the Holy Spirit directed me to sing a different song from the one that I had prepared.

I opened my mouth and looked at the large congregation, knowing that if nothing happened I could always sit down after an apology. To my surprise, I heard the most beautiful voice come out of my mouth. Never had I sung like this before. It was ministering to me and tears were flowing from my eyes and also from the eyes of many people in the congregation.

The moment I finished singing there was an awesome sense of power and the presence of the Lord, and people started to walk forward to be prayed for to have their lives sorted out. The Sunday School teachers came back into the church after their classes had finished and I was asked, "What had happened in the service, because we could feel the power of God in the adjoining rooms and what have we therefore missed?"

As I tried to answer I still had no voice! This all happened because I sang in faith, with no musical instrument and with no voice, the song that the Lord had given to me.

HARPING ON ABOUT IT

'Then I will praise you with music on the harp.' (Psalm 71 v 22a)

I had always longed to play a full-sized harp.

Still in mission work, we were invited by an expatriate American businessman and his wife to spend the day with them. They lived in one of the jungle villages that had to be accessed by a very small boat on the river, in view of his involvement in the oil industry. At their house you can imagine my astonishment and delight when the wife enquired, "Would you like to see my harp and perhaps you might like to play it?"

I tried to hide my excitement as I tackled this full-sized harp! But how wonderful to praise God in a similar way to King David so long ago.

It was a dream come true and of course amazing. Please don't think every jungle home comes complete with a huge harp, but I must say, even here in the U.K., the opportunity has never presented itself to me again.

MUSICAL MIRACLE

'Praise the Lord! Sing to the Lord a new song. Sing His praises in the assembly of the faithful.' (Psalm 149 v 1)

At one time the Lord told my husband and I to meet together in our home and that others would join us, which is what happened. We worshipped, prayed and studied the Bible together.

Our ministry had been to pioneer and build up and encourage other churches and groups so we were excited at what the Lord was now telling us to do.

However, in the beginning we had to be sure that we had heard from the Lord correctly. We received confirmation of this when a friend rang up to say that God had instructed him to tell us, "To continue doing what you are doing."

In the course of time we felt it right to join with another couple who were pioneering a new church and soon the meeting in our house became the midweek church meeting.

As the original group grew, the need for a proper musical instrument became a priority and, after prayer, my husband believed that God would have us go to a particular music shop and that, once there, God would guide us as to what we should buy. This would be interesting as we only had a limited budget set aside for this purpose!

At the time, the little Rolf Harris stylophones were very popular and, although small, they sounded good and I thought I might be able to master one as, in the absence of anyone else, I would probably have to play. The cost of this instrument was within our budget.

The manager listened to our story and showed me a larger stylophone, one which I did not know existed. Meantime, my husband had been wandering around the shop and came rushing over to me, quite excitedly. "The Lord has shown me that we are to buy this keyboard." It was expensive and not something my careful husband would ordinarily have proffered. If we didn't know how to pay for such an instrument, it really didn't matter what price it was, I reasoned. I looked across at my husband and caught his excitement. The Lord had suddenly reminded him that he had received a tax rebate in the post that very morning, and yes, it was ex*actly* the price of the keyboard! Isn't God amazing?

It had been a wonderful witness to the manager of the shop. We came home and my husband assembled the instrument. "Did the Lord tell you who would play it?" I asked. "Yes, *you*," he answered. I did not know how to play it but expectant in faith by now, I placed my hands on the keys and I was amazed at the miracle. I had never before experienced what happened as I found I could play without any tuition whatsoever!

The keyboard eventually went on to bless others. God gave it. God moved it on.

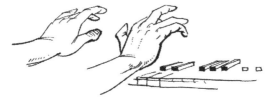

WITNESS EVERYWHERE

'If you are asked about your Christian hope, always be ready to explain it.'   (1 Peter 3 v 15b)

A friend and I were lunching at a country pub when the Holy Spirit began to move on me to write down the words of a song that He had started to give to me. It's called, 'Oh the love of God' and the words follow:

OH THE LOVE OF GOD.

Oh the love of God is reaching out to you.
The precious love of God, you know the love is true.
His love will never let you down or let you go.
The tender love of God is more than you can know.

> *Receive the love of God, He's reaching out to you*
> *Believe the love of God, there's nothing else to do.*
> *Just open up your heart He'll fill the deepest part*
> *Receive the love of God He's reaching out to you.*

The Spirit's moving now, your love for Him He'll win.
His power is flowing now to fill you deep within.
Just lift up holy hands and glorify His name
Receive the love of God and overflow again.

> *Oh the love of God, it reaches every shore.*
> *The precious love of God flows deeper than before.*
> *So share the love of God to everyone around,*
> *The pain, the suffering His touch through you breaks down.*

He'll heal the broken heart and set the captive free.
His love and power within will give you victory.
He'll make the lame to walk and cause the blind to see.
The Spirit's touch refreshing you and me.

> *The steadfast love of God is faithful every day.*
> *His mercies ever new. His grace will guide the way.*
> *Just see how much His love will keep you in His care.*
> *The precious love of God is always, always there.*

Rebekkah Clark

Oh the deep, deep love, the love that never fails.
Believe the word of God and all His truth entails.
His love will never let you run or let you hide.
If you make your bed in hell He'll still be by your side.

He'll take you on my friend to great heights with Him.
And if your heart is still you'll know His voice within.
He'll show you deepest love in ways you'll understand.
So put your trust in Him, you're in His perfect plan.

While we were talking and writing the publican was watching us with apparent interest.

God obviously knew what he was doing as the publican soon came over to our table and enquired if he could get us anything else. To our surprise he seemed to take a real interest and asked what it was I was writing.

When I explained, he expressed that he had noticed that there was 'something different' about us. He asked to hear more and was there time for him to go and fetch his wife who was resting upstairs, which he did. We were able to explain to them both about the love of God.

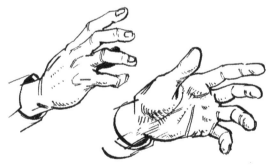

It wasn't long before they resigned from that job and moved on elsewhere. Could it be that they experienced for themselves the love of God and that He had moved them in a new direction?

UNITY PRESERVED

'Holy Father, keep them and care for them - all those you have
given me – so that they will be united just as we are.' (John 17 v 11b)

It was in the middle of the service. Here I was visiting a church and I felt the anointing of the Holy Spirit strong upon me. He was urging me to get up and speak the words He was giving me. "You just don't *do* that kind of thing," I reasoned with myself. I *could* just pretend I hadn't noticed the Holy Spirit's unction. I knew better. I stood to my feet and began to speak words. I then started to sing – "If your heart is right with my heart give me your hand."

You could have heard a pin drop. I walked up to people with my arm outstretched as I continued to sing. People shuffled and turned their faces away, looking deeply hurt. "Everyone leave your seats and come stand in a circle together. Take the hand of anyone with whom you are out of fellowship," I said. Then I started to sing, "Let there be love shared among us." Repentant hearts started to weep.

The church had never had a meeting like it but everyone realized that God had spoken and they responded as they felt they should.

One of the leaders stood to his feet. He spoke to my husband and myself advising us that there had been a meeting just the day before trying to decide whether or not to close down the church. The reason? Such disunity. Divisions caused by those that thought they knew better than God's appointed leaders. Whatever the Lord had spoken through me was clearly directional for that church. The closure never took place! Praise His Name!

MY CO-WORKER

'Sing a new song to the Lord!'   (Psalm 96 v 1a)

A lady joined the church that we were attending and soon afterwards approached my husband to ask if she could attend the House Group we were running. The group was an interesting mix as described in Chapter One, 'This is Church folks.' It was good to have someone who was a real asset and who would make a positive contribution.

She loved the Word of God and over a period of time a close, strong and deep friendship developed, the like of which I had never known before, and may possibly never again. We were so different, yet so in tune. My extrovert personality balanced her introverted nature. She wasn't always quiet though and could be the life and soul of the party at times.

She is an amazing Bible teacher, and the Lord shows her things which are truly a revelation. She also has a tremendous knowledge that just pours out from her. She would say that my personality helped draw out of her what she was very often unaware of herself.

We often drove along together, listening to a teaching tape. We never progressed far with it, because we kept stopping it to discuss points. From this amazing friendship came the writing of songs. Usually she wrote the words and I composed the melody, but not always. With the anointing there, we would even go away for weekends to write these songs without home distractions.

On one particular occasion we attended a wedding quite some distance away. There we met the person who was to become our musical director and we travelled many miles to his studio to put our first recording together.

It was such a feeling of accomplishment and she was a great support in believing in my singing ability, which was an insecure area for me. We knew times of wonderful fellowship with the Lord.

Further recordings were made, some of which were later put onto a CD for us.

These are two of the songs, which in this case, the Lord gave to *me*.

FATHER I NEED TO TALK TO YOU

Father I need to talk to you,
Father I need to say,
My life isn't all it ought to be
And I've really had a bad day.
I need to know you are here, Lord,
Just feel you loving me.
I have opened up my heart and my ears, Lord,
Now I can hear you say:

My child don't despair,
I am always very near
And I'll never let you fall away.
My child don't despair,
I am always very near
And I'll never let you fall away.

This second song was written out of my counselling experience and has spoken to many a person who had thought they had fallen too far and that God was not interested in their situation

I'M SEARCHING FOR A LIFE OF HOPE

I'm searching for a life of hope when in this world I find no one who'll bear my sorrows, heal my wounds because it seems, there's only dreams and despair.

Where people turn to sex and dope, to find their peace through life they grope, I look right up, beyond the sky, I ponder there and wonder why. When I'm alone.

I cry for help, but no one hears. I stretch my hands and reach for hope. Is there a God and does he care, and can I feel Him everywhere? Please tell me.

There is no one whom I can love. Is there a God in heaven above who loves me? I put the tablets right away; the needle in the drawer would stay, if He would help me.

If He would come right near to me. I'd touch His hands, my tears He'd see and understand. There is no more that I can do, I hand my life over to You, can You hear me?

My child, I am the living God and I have heard your cries and I will heal your pain.
To bear away your sin, yes I am really here.
I'm risen now at God's right-hand, preparing a place for you to stand with me.

I'll put my love within your heart if in return you'll give your will to me.
My child I will forgive your sin,
If you repent right now, I'll send my angels down to dry away your tears, my child, just trust me.

My Holy Spirit, He will lead you into truth and then you'll see, I love you.
So trust me child, all mine is yours, you need not search again in vain.
Please love me. Please love me. Please love me.

Please love me, please love me.
Please love me, please love me.
Please love me, please love me.

Chapter 5

NEEDS SATISFIED

Bargain wash

Washday challenge

That's stretching it don't you think?

My coat

Supernatural isn't the word

Miracles with the weather

Think of a number

Care prayer

BARGAIN WASH

'Abraham named the place "The Lord Will Provide." This name has now become a proverb: "On the mountain of the Lord it will be provided."' (Genesis 22 v 14)

We'd just returned from the mission field and used what money we had as a down payment on a house. Most modern appliances would simply have to wait, even down to basics like a vacuum cleaner and a washing machine.

Our ten-month old baby kept me busy with piles of nappies to wash. Those were *not* the days of the convenient throwaway type. There was a muslin *and* a towelling one to tackle each time. After they soaked in a bucket, I placed them in the sink and scrubbed away on a washboard. It was not a great success and so I had a go at putting the galvanised bucket on the electric cooking ring. There was always a risk that the cooker enamel would get damaged but I had to boil the nappies somehow. It was simply something that I had to get on with.

We settled into a church as soon as possible and a kind lady there offered me her baby Burco. What luxury – just plug it in and away we go. Twice the size of the bucket as well! Was I grateful!

Everything was fine but by now I had a second child and on one occasion she came crawling into the kitchen just as the little boiler decided to bubble over, with hot soapy water. I managed to snatch my baby back in time but now realized the practical difficulties I had.

Sometime later, we were visiting my mother (bus, train, bags and two toddlers) when her neighbour happened to ask us if we would like a washing machine for £5.00. It was a lot of money for us, but still cheap, even in 1964. The neighbour worked for a company that sold washing machines and had decided to sell off two large, cumbersome, top-loaders, complete with ugly wringers on top. He eventually sent us both for £9.00, the idea being that we could keep the second for spares.

We accepted delightedly and looked forward to their delivery. The spare was put in the shed and the one in the kitchen took up all of the space but who cared? It met a great need. I would move everything around somehow. The day my first load of washing went in and came out so beautifully white made it all worthwhile. I even enjoyed using the wringer and having faster drying time. I now knew what the expression 'going through the wringer' meant! I had more time too – no more having to have the nappies out on the line by 6.00am to be ready for use the next day. It made a huge difference with our white cotton sheets too! Bliss!

Some while later, a friend of my husband told us that his mother's washing machine had had to be scrapped and she could not afford to buy a new one. We were delighted to be able to offer our second one (still in the shed) to this lady, which she gladly accepted. It lasted for several years.

Two washing machines – and for just nine pounds? I hadn't even put my need in prayer, and yet God still mightily provided for us, and in the three years we had the machine, it *never* required maintenance! This reminded me of the children of Israel in the desert – their shoes and clothes never wore out.

Eventually we part exchanged our machine for £10!

WASHDAY CHALLENGE

'And this same God who takes care of me will supply all your needs from His glorious riches, which have been given to us in Christ Jesus.' (Philippians 4 v 19)

Did you ever own an upright washing machine? Come on own up! Wonderful invention! Easily accessible for pulling out any drip-dry items for hand rinsing and hanging whilst others continued the circuit! I was proud of my model and I didn't want to exchange it for the current front-loaders on offer.

At the time (1981) I had just waved goodbye to a number of friends who had been staying with us over the weekend. I stripped the beds and loaded my trusty machine. I switched it on and nothing happened. Oh no! What shall I do? Okay – in everything give thanks. I kept singing and praising joyfully anyway, not wanting to lose the benefit of our good time together.

I started to scrub away by hand at the sink and found my English praise had progressed to tongues. I was offering the situation to the Lord, yet mentally wondering how the machine could be repaired when I had no money and it was obsolete. My train of thought found me considering what other appliances I might be able to do without? Iron, vacuum cleaner, washing machine, washing line – funny, as they are all connected in the cleanliness cycle. Then I switched track and thought about extras such as a spin dryer.

Water was by now everywhere because I was wringing out huge sheets by hand! Still praising *I* realised that five numbers kept coming to mind. Could they be a telephone number?

Hands dried, I reached for the phone. A voice answered, "Washing Machine Repairs, how can I help you?" I put on my boldest voice and explained the problem and the type of machine. A mechanic was soon on the way and upon arrival he diagnosed the machine to be 'dead.' "The casing is very good though!"

Rebekkah Clark

As I continued hand washing at the sink another set of numbers came into my head. Could this be God gaining my attention again, I wondered. I rang the number and found it was a church acquaintance. After the usual pleasantries she suddenly enquired if I might need a spin-dryer, which was taking up unnecessary space in the loft! Praise the Lord. He answered before I even framed my thoughts into a prayer.

Returning to my washing, my thoughts went to my husband. He'd also gone off to the office that morning with problems – the huge financial variety! As he left, he muttered that we might have to move house and maybe have to take our three girls out of their private school. The ringing of the telephone interrupted me. It was the Washing Machine Mechanic calling back with some incredible news!

"You'll never guess, I've just had a call from a customer who emigrated six months ago to Australia! She'd just remembered that she'd left a washing machine with me for repair and it's still here. She asked me if I knew of anyone who might like it – no charge. Better still, it's the same type of washing machine as yours and although the cabinet is very poor the working parts are all good. I can call round and do a switchover for you!"

I was speechless! Practically a new machine, still of my preferred upright variety at no cost, with a spin-dryer thrown in too! Isn't God terrific?

I was that excited that I hardly gave my husband a chance to speak when he came through the door. He insisted that I first listen to his own miracle. Although an Accountant, well used to handling finances and helping others out of difficulties, he could see no way out of his own recession-induced situation. He was willing to resign his job if it became necessary. However, his boss had shown him a workable way through, resulting in a better deal all round, with even some cash spare to settle a debt.

When I poured out my good news too, we just rejoiced and praised the Lord for His marvellous goodness.

THAT'S STRETCHING IT
DON'T YOU THINK?

'Jesus looked at them intently and said, "Humanly speaking, it is impossible. But with God everything is possible."' (Matthew 19 v 26)

My husband and I were invited to a couple's home one time when they had just purchased a new bath for the cottage that they were renovating. Nothing unusual about that except that the bathroom was tiny and the bath, although the smallest they could find, just would not fit into place. This obviously called for a miracle and we knew who could provide this, as with God all things are possible.

The couple found tremendous faith welling up in them and we agreed with them in prayer, asking the Lord either to stretch the walls or shrink the bath – whichever He chose! Then once again the bath was tried and, amazingly it simply slotted into place.

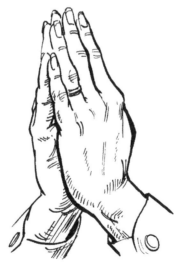

We danced and praised the Lord, although I secretly wanted to know which option God had used, but I never did find out. Praise Him however that he cares about our every need and no minute detail is overlooked.

I later noticed that the toilet was now touching the bath. A little correction needed here. My faith was much encouraged so I asked the Lord to move things around a little – and He did!

The encounter with this couple had a much wider effect than what had happened. For we got to know them very well and I understood and was able to pass on to them the fact that God had far greater plans for them, as a couple, than they had thought possible.

MY COAT

'They gave to anyone as he had need.' (Acts 2 v 45b NIV)

I was going out and reached for my favourite coat. Just as I was putting it on the Lord spoke to my spirit, "I want you to take the coat and give it to a certain friend." I was astonished and tried to ignore what I had heard. That quiet persistent voice was still there, waiting for my obedience. This was difficult for me, but nevertheless I took the coat and made my way to her house.

"Perhaps she's out," I hoped as I rang the doorbell. Almost immediately the door opened and there stood the person so I offered her my coat. "Oh!" she exclaimed. "I've just been praying for a coat and this is exactly the one I wanted! That's the quickest answer to prayer I've ever had! Thank you so much." She was so excited, she almost snatched it out of my hands as she closed the door. I walked away, without 'my' coat.

I should have been thrilled, yet somehow I felt the loss. The Lord was dealing with me and bringing me to a place where I wouldn't hold on tightly to anything of this world.

It's not as though I wasn't a liberal tither, or a giver. I disappointed myself. I realised that this was a different lesson to be learnt. God didn't mind me having possessions as long as the possessions didn't have me! I had to remember this each time I saw 'my' coat being worn by that friend!

SUPERNATURAL ISN'T THE WORD

'The Lord said to Moses, "Come up to me on the mountain."'
(Exodus 24 v 12a)

We had driven up the mountain road to the top of the Alps with mountains as far as the eye could see. Marvellous spectacle. Suddenly the fan belt snapped in our Audi. We managed to freewheel to a passing place, where we saw a man picking berries. We tried to show him our problem, using our very best sign language. It must have worked because he suddenly disappeared into the boot of his own car and proudly produced the very fan belt that we needed for the Audi! He kindly offered it to us and refused any payment. That was fine, but neither of us had the necessary tool to remove the alternator in order to replace the fan belt.

So, we continued to freewheel down the mountain when, to our amazement number two, we came upon a small petrol station and garage. Who this garage served up there in the Alps was far from clear!

We indicated our problem to the lady petrol attendant, but she refused to unlock the garage workshop at the rear. It had closed just half an hour previously for the weekend. We could see the very tool through the window and we tried for a quarter of an hour to persuade her to change her mind, with the help of a French woman who was interpreting for us.

Then a man appeared who had been repairing his own car round the back of the garage and who must have overheard the proceedings. He came over to us and produced his own tool and even replaced the fan belt for us. My husband's clothes were by now grease-ruined, but we continued our journey without further mishap. As we travelled, we reflected on what had just taken place and how it was that a garage was lodged so high up in the Alps!

Back in England some time later, the car had to go in for a service. My husband idly mentioned 'the Alps incident' to the mechanic who remarked, "I'm sure if you went back today, there'd be no garage there!"

God's ways are certainly higher than ours and His timing is perfect. The garage and the people were almost certainly placed there for our benefit according to God's purposes, planned before the foundation of the world.

Supernatural isn't the word!

MIRACLES WITH THE WEATHER

'Now Elijah, who was from Tishbe in Gilead, told King Ahab, "As surely as the Lord, the God of Israel, lives - the God whom I worship and serve - there will be no dew or rain during the next few years unless I give the word!"' (I Kings 17 v 1)

Having decided to try out his faith on the weather my husband had been encouraged with positive results on numerous occasions.

One example was the day we were taking a number of children and their parents to a large theme park. The weather forecast had been grim, indeed it was already raining heavily when everyone gathered at the beginning of the day. Nevertheless that very morning the Lord had given my husband confirmation of good weather from the Scriptures in 1 Kings 17 v 1 as set out above.

The children started to board the coaches, but many of the parents were quite apprehensive. Most understandably as the sky was black, with thunder, lightning and torrential rain pouring down from the sky. In addition, it was very cold and blustery.

One of the coach drivers was Job's comforter himself and thought we were mad but my husband assured him that the weather would be fine at the theme park. The children were keen to make a start for they hadn't contemplated what it might be like at the other end. We set off and the weather didn't improve at all on the journey.

However, when we arrived, right above the park there was blue sky! It was sunny and dry underfoot whereas all around the perimeter of the park it was pouring with rain. The coach drivers came in as well and also enjoyed the sunshine for the whole day along with the rest of us. This must have given them some food for thought!

But the moment that we left the park, the skies opened up and rain beat down upon the coaches, continuing all the way to the church hall, in a nearby town, where tea had been prepared for us by helpers who had not come to the theme park.

We were met with many a sympathetic comment, as despite the fact that it was only seven miles away, it had poured with rain there for the whole day. My husband thanked God that his prayer of faith had been answered and for the wonderful day we had all enjoyed. Even the coach driver commented, during the homeward journey, that it had been truly amazing!

One of our neighbours on hearing of my husband's faith in praying for good weather asked if he would pray for the sun to shine on their son's wedding day, as the forecast was grim. When we awoke on the morning of the wedding, there were blue skies and it was gloriously hot and the wedding took place in glorious weather. Praise the Lord!

THINK OF A NUMBER

'Now glory be to God! By His mighty power at work within us, He is able to accomplish infinitely more than we would ever dare to ask or hope.' (Ephesians 3v20)

It was approaching our middle daughter's eighteenth birthday. She asked if she could hold a party in our home for a few people. Sixty-six to be precise! Her father explained the practical impossibilities of such a number and asked her to cut back. We had first-hand experience of the exact number of people that our home could comfortably hold, as we had often held youth meetings in it. Half that number would still mean that people would need to be packed in and would be quite impractical for a party.

My husband had a sudden inspiration as he announced that he would pray that the day would be blessed with wonderful weather so that the party could be held outside in the garden! April had been known to produce a few surprises in years past, I confidently told myself.

Meanwhile, our daughter did manage to eliminate six guests, but suddenly remembered six other very important ones that had been overlooked, and so it remained at the original total. "Let them come," said my husband, fully confident in his ability to pray for good weather. Both of us wanted it to go well for her.

Came the morning and my husband swept the patio and prepared everything for the outdoor party. Looking good. Five pm. arrived – and it began to rain. "Just a short shower. Rain will be gone before guests arrive," said my husband, "Just a test." By seven o'clock it had started snowing! Guests began arriving at eight o'clock. I glanced down at the girls' stilettos – there was by now a foot of snow on the ground but somehow they had managed to scramble up the driveway steps to enter the house.

Once everyone was safely indoors we all enjoyed a wonderfully successful party.

None of us gave a second thought that everything took place indoors, but the next morning my husband remembered his prayer and questioned the Lord about the weather. The answer came, "That was not your problem, you needed to house sixty six people and I answered your prayer exactly." God had done it – we don't know precisely how; had the walls been stretched, or had the people been shrunk? God was able to give our daughter His own present, and do it in real supernatural style, as someone actually remarked, "There was room for another twenty people in the house that evening."

Just as a by the way, the following week we hosted a youth fellowship meeting in our home and everyone had a job to move freely with half the number that had attended the party!

Think of a number – and God will double it!

CARE PRAYER

'Give all your worries and cares to God, for He cares about what happens to you.' (I Peter 5 v 7)

I had a 'phone call from a friend. She was in dire need of help, having fallen awkwardly in the bath. She had managed to haul herself out and crawl to the 'phone to ring me. I went to her and managed to ease her onto a mattress on the floor and care for her until an ambulance arrived.

She was in hospital for a long while because of complications that followed an operation she had to undergo. I prayed that she would have a Christian nurse in attendance who would be able to talk to her about the Lord and build on what I had shared with her over the years.

I later found out from a pastor that an off-duty nurse from his congregation had felt led by the Lord to go and speak to her. She had prayed with her and led her to the Lord. He cares for each and every person.

Chapter 6

ANGELIC ENCOUNTERS

When Angels came to visit

Faith to live by

A voice from heaven

Another time, another place

Whoops

Angels on assignment

Vive Espana

Amazing or what?

WHEN ANGELS CAME TO VISIT

'Suddenly, the angel was joined by a vast host of others - the armies of heaven - praising God: "Glory to God in the highest heaven, and peace on earth to whom all God favours."' (Luke 2 v 13,14)

The pen friend of one of our daughters had visited us in the previous year. We had lately been through a very traumatic time. A fire in our house had completely gutted it, causing us to have to rent a property elsewhere whilst the house was being refurbished. In view of this the pen friend's parents had kindly invited us spend a holiday with them in Germany. We accepted gratefully.

On arrival, we were all shown to our respective rooms. The children were on the second floor and we were to be in the brand new loft conversion. It was absolutely beautifully furnished, a bedroom-cum-study. The room was in an L-shape and arranged with two single beds, one placed under the window and the other along the side wall.

That night, after my husband and I had prayed, he fell asleep almost immediately. I was still awake in the side wall bed, and became disturbed in my spirit about something in the room. I got up and went over to the study area, where I found shelves of statues and effigies from Africa. Our host obviously collected them. I knew they were not evil in themselves and were not used for any sinister purpose, but still felt no peace in the room. I concluded that there must have been an object among them that had some evil association. I sat on the edge of my bed and asked the Lord to deal with whatever was in that room and to restore my peace, allowing me to sense His Presence. Into my mind came the words of a song, "I heard the angels sing, Glory Hallelujah. A mighty chorus way up high."

Immediately the window above my husband's bed opened and the curtains were blowing and I heard the most beautiful sound. Music seemed to be coming from a distance, perhaps the end of the road, and it was getting closer. A choir of male voices was becoming louder by the second. I thought it might wake up the entire household, perhaps even the neighbourhood. But I was wrong. My husband continued to sleep soundly and heard nothing.

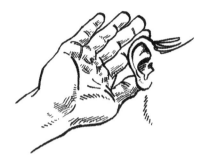

The heavenly voices came through the window and into the room, enveloping me completely. I simply sat and listened as they ministered to my spirit. When they left, I knew peace had been so sweetly restored to me. All sense of evil had been driven out by their all-pervading presence. The window closed and I pinched myself to make sure I wasn't dreaming. My husband woke and asked me why I was sitting on the edge of the bed. I told him everything and he was then sad to have missed the heavenly visitation.

He did have the privilege of worshipping with angels at a later date. We were at a house-group meeting which we were leading and on this particular occasion, only seven of us were present. I was leading worship when we suddenly realised that there were hundreds of voices singing along with us! We were very moved and awestruck by what was happening and we worshipped with the angels for at least a quarter of an hour. Then we went to prayer.

The following day, a neighbour of the host in whose house we had met, remarked to her, "Who were all the people that arrived at your house last night and how did you manage to get them all in, because I saw them? The singing was also very loud and very sweet." She confirmed what we had experienced. The host was able to explain that although there were only seven of us present we had been blessed with a visitation of angels.

On three other occasions we have also had the joy of angels singing with us in our gatherings.

FAITH TO LIVE BY

'I pray that you will begin to understand the incredible greatness of His power for us who believe Him.' (Ephesians 1 v 19)

The school secretary rang to say that one of my daughters was unwell and needed me to pick her up. I left the house in a hurry and later realised I still had my slippers on! I collected my daughter and began the journey home.

Going through town, I glanced across at a bus-stop and recognised somebody from our church. He was holding his jaw and looked to be in a bad way. I stopped and asked him if he was all right and he explained that he had been to the dentist and was in a lot of pain and was anxious to get home as soon as possible.

I offered him a lift and took the shortest route to his house. I don't know if this was helpful as my shortcut took us down a private road, complete with road humps. The humps probably added more to the man's discomfort! We delivered him safely home and then proceeded to return the same way. A short distance along the private road to my amazement, the gear stick just fell flat onto the floor of the car! (I am not certain to this day whether or not it snapped.) The car juddered to a halt in second gear.

At the time I had been listening to an audiotape I'd recently been given. It was by a man well-known in Christian circles who gave remarkable accounts of supernatural events which spurred me into faith (and I hope to do the same for you with the writing of this book).

I looked across at my daughter, who was herself wanting to get home, and I remembered that I was still in my slippers. The prospect of walking the long distance home in these did not appeal to me. However, I took courage from what I'd been hearing, and 'faith' Scriptures began to pop into my thoughts. 'Where does faith come from? Faith comes by hearing and hearing comes from the Word of God.' Also, 'Without faith it is impossible to please God.'

I recalled one of the man's stories when he was in a similar situation. Like him, I commanded the car to start, in Jesus' Name. Amazingly, the car moved forward and, without my touching the steering wheel, took us home – supernaturally! My heart lurched as we travelled over the humps at tremendous speed. I knew there was a T-junction ahead and I remember shouting, "Lord, left at the T-junction!"

Soon the car slowed and rested nicely on our driveway! My husband came out to greet us. He had been working at home and I recounted to him what had happened. We praised the Lord for His wonderful, supernatural intervention and protection in getting us home. Those angels sure know how to drive!

We still needed to have the car repaired. The Lord expects us to do what we can for ourselves.

A similar incident occurred when on another occasion I ran out of petrol, and the Lord got us safely home, but I still needed to fill the car the next day.

A VOICE FROM HEAVEN

' He fell to the ground and heard a voice.' (Acts 9v 4a)

A couple were returning from Liverpool after having delivered a package. The wife was driving the van and her husband was taking a nap. "Brake!" said a sudden voice. She ignored it. "Brake!" said the voice again. Still she took no notice and carried on driving. "Brake!" said the voice for the third time, this time with such great urgency that she responded. At that moment an approaching juggernaut jack-knifed and had they not stopped they would most certainly have been killed.

As the van jerked to a halt, her husband had been shaken awake. He had seen what was happening and was completely astounded. She was so grateful that he had shouted to her and made her brake. "I never said a word," he replied, "I was asleep!"

The next day I was leading a Ladies Bible study on the subject of angels. The doorbell suddenly rang and I heard one of the ladies explaining to the caller that we were otherwise engaged. Nevertheless this visitor came into the room after the hostess had checked with me that she could interrupt the Bible study. It was the lady who had heard the word 'Brake' and she wanted to ask if we could explain her experience.

None of her neighbours had been able to explain where the word had come from, but one had indicated that our Bible study hostess was a Christian and she might be able to help.

We listened to her story and I was able to tell her that I believed that she had heard an angel of God protecting her husband and herself and thus giving them the opportunity of hearing about and coming into the Kingdom of God.

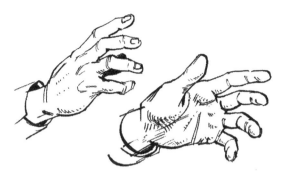

There were many problems in their lives and they often had heated arguments. Most of these were because they had not been able to have children as the wife had suffered six miscarriages all at six weeks. I said, "You won't lose the seventh child."

Amazingly she was already pregnant again and she was in her sixth week! We all prayed that this baby would come to full term and be delivered healthily. This happened and she called her son, Samuel. Praise the Lord!

The lady gave her life to Jesus the very next day and a few weeks later her husband did the same. She later gave birth to two more perfect children.

ANOTHER TIME,
ANOTHER PLACE

'I pray that your hearts will be flooded with light so that you can understand the wonderful future He has promised to those He called. I want you to realize what a rich and glorious inheritance He has given to His people.' (Ephesians 1 v 18)

Our country travel routine quickly became established – my husband preached and I sang. I never looked for opportunities, but it seemed God was there ahead of me whatever time, whatever place we happened to visit.

On one occasion we decided we needed a well-earned rest and opted to go away for a quiet weekend! We were in the area of a church that had seen God move for over a decade. They had just a small congregation but there was anointing there and many people had been helped when they had visited. Visitors had caught the anointing and had taken it back to their own churches.

We wanted somewhere to worship over the weekend and my husband suggested that we visit this particular church. As we entered, he said, "Let's just take a back seat and enjoy what the Lord wants to do and be blessed." I was in full agreement, after all, we *were* on a short holiday. Why then did I sense that there was something terribly wrong in the church? I relayed this to my husband and he emphasised the fact that we were just here on our break. "No problem," I assured him, "I simply sensed there is something not right."

The service began but seemed to struggle to get off the ground. The opposite was true of me! The Holy Spirit yanked me up to prophecy but I could see my husband wanting the floor to open up and swallow him! Can I help it that God doesn't take a holiday?

I rely on my husband to make sure I am moving in the Spirit but it took me back a bit when he exclaimed, "Do you know what you have just said?" I admitted I didn't as I simply opened my mouth and the Lord spoke through me.

Just then, the senior elder of the church stood to his feet. He was a well-known figure in Christian circles, a man with a healing ministry. He revealed that the church had not been moving in power as it once did. He himself had lost confidence in his ability to minister in the healing power of the Lord since his sister had died from cancer. He said that they had been considering closing down the work but was grateful that the Lord had spoken into the situation through me.

I was completely unaware of the circumstances, but God had spoken directly into this man's life and into the future of the church. Just then, a beautiful Holy-Spirit empowered voice left my lips. I was singing a new song in the Spirit and was ushered to the front so that the pianist could pick it up and play, as the Holy Spirit taught the words.

People in the congregation began to sing the song and some got up to dance around the church. The leader confessed that this had not happened for a very long time because they had lost sight of the God they once knew. However, it seemed that the Holy Spirit was pouring out grace upon the people again as they renewed their walk with Him.

Mine is a very unusual ministry in many ways. Such directional prophecy has to be checked to ensure that it IS from God! Many people think that they have a 'word from the Lord' but it is often their own human prompting. There has to be a definite Holy Spirit anointing before moving out in this area.

It was here that I learnt that prophetic utterances can be a challenge as well as encouraging.

WHOOPS

'They (angels) will hold you with their hands to keep you from striking your foot on a stone.' (Psalm 91 v 12)

This'll make you laugh! I stepped out of my front door on one occasion and events just kind of 'overtook me.' I was unaware of black ice and skidded over the step, sliding down a precarious sloping path, over an equally sloping grassy bank, landing on my rear in an ungainly manner, right in front of our local milk float which had just come to a halt. There is always someone around when you don't want them to be!

I tried to gain my composure and stand up as though nothing had happened. "Excuse me," I murmured as I turned and went back very carefully into the house. It was only when the milkman called out, "Are you all right?" that I realised what an escapade that was! I had travelled twenty-five feet without incurring damage to mind, spirit or body. I pondered – could an angel have carried me?

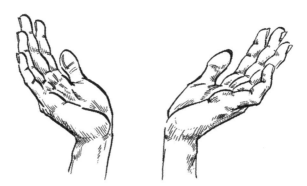

ANGELS ON ASSIGNMENT

'In the sixth month of Elizabeth's pregnancy, God sent the angel Gabriel to Nazareth, a village in Galilee.' (Luke 1 v 26)

Any one of my daughters could bring someone home to stay the night without asking, so it was a surprise when one of them asked if a friend could stay. It was a pleasure to say yes. During the evening the two girls went to my daughter's bedroom and after a while I was called to pray for the friend who was deeply troubled.

Her father was extremely ill and she had just learned that he was suffering from cancer. She stayed the night and, when I asked, said that her father would be at home the following day as he was now unable to go to work.

The next evening my husband and I went to see her father and his wife to pray for him. We were gratefully received and the man explained the doctor's diagnosis and pointed to the protruding lump in his intestine. It was bigger than a tennis ball and clearly visible through his clothes. The doctor's prognosis was that the growth was now beyond operation and that there was little hope of recovery. My husband laid hands on the man and we both prayed for him.

 He was due to see the specialist again the next day and was expecting to be kept in hospital. I just knew however that our prayers had been answered and that he was going to be fine although I didn't ask him to verify things at that time.

My husband and I went home in great peace, yet that night I felt led to pray that the Angel Gabriel would take that man by the hand as he crossed the threshold of the hospital. I did not understand why but knew I was being directed by the Holy Spirit.

The next day I decided to go and see how he was. My daughter's friend answered the door and whilst I was sitting having coffee with her I asked if she knew how things had gone at the hospital. I had already looked around and noticed that her father was not at home.

With tremendous excitement she told me that her father had returned to work! She filled me in with the details and I later heard all about it from the man himself! He had arrived at the hospital in much trepidation, knowing that he might never leave it alive. He got as far as the hospital door and then felt very nervous and was unable to go in, so he just stood at the threshold on the steps, immobilised. He told me that at this point he cried out to God and then amazingly, the Angel Gabriel appeared and took him by the hand, walking him into the hospital and accompanying him to see the specialist.

He was examined and yes, that lump had completely disappeared. An X-ray showed that he was completely clear of cancer, and so he had decided that there was only one thing to do – go back to work!

Rebekkah Clark

VIVE ESPANA

'For He orders His angels to protect you wherever you go.' *(Psalm 91 v 11)*

We were off the boat and on our way at last. Teaching tapes in our walkmans, my friend and I settled down in the back of the car, enjoying being driven to our Spanish holiday villa by my husband.

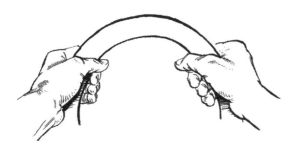

The hot afternoon sun streamed in through the windows, and we smiled at the soft hum of the air-conditioning keeping us cool and protected from it's effects. Two weeks of Mediterranean pampering lay ahead. We drifted off into cosy oblivion.

My senses were suddenly alerted. I looked up to see that the car was veering at full motorway speed towards a walled crash barrier. I thought my husband was pulling over into a lay-by but then I realized that he had fallen asleep at the wheel. I cried out, " Jesus!" Flying glass and dirt filled the car as it made contact with the wall but thankfully my sunglasses protected my eyes. The car skimmed along the wall for some distance before finally grinding to a grimy halt. The right-hand doors were jammed and buckled, the windows no longer existed. A mangled, tangled mess that only minutes before was our holiday transport.

Shaken and covered in debris, we tried to scramble out of the car from the left side, taking care as this was on the side of the motorway. I had received most of the impact of the flying glass and was covered in cuts and scratches, and I had also banged my mouth on the seat in front as my head had been flung forward. However, for the most part, injuries were superficial. We had escaped almost unscathed and somehow knew that a miracle had taken place. The car had actually been turned and a head-on collision, with possibly tragic results, had been avoided. In fact, the car skimmed the barrier wall until it ground to a standstill, as though having run out of breath. To this day I believe it to have been the ministry of angels in attendance who turned the car at my cry of "Jesus!"

Now fully awake, my husband, unhurt but shaken, made off to try and find a telephone box and get some police assistance. Eventually, after what seemed like a lifetime, police and ambulance arrived. Their first question was, "Where are the bodies?" My husband had not yet returned and the police were searching everywhere, believing the driver to have been ejected and killed. Such was the condition of the wrecked vehicle. No one would believe that we had all escaped virtually unharmed and it took some persuading to convince them that we *were* the passengers.

So you see – I *do* believe in miracles. I was part *of* one.

Rebekkah Clark

AMAZING OR WHAT?

*'One night the Lord spoke to Paul in a vision and told him, "Don't
be afraid! Speak out! Don't be silent!"' (Acts 18 v 9)*

I think that the way the Lord uses people is at times nothing short
of amazing. You just couldn't 'dream up' some of His methods. I'd
never heard anyone share anything like some of the ways God has
directed me and so I was very reluctant to share with anyone, for a
long time.

Last thing at night, my husband and I always prayed together, after
which he would go to sleep almost immediately. I would often lie
in bed with my eyes closed and in my mind see a scene, often like a
movie, unfold before me. I would see the whole scenario and know
where it was and even in which country. I knew it was a prompt to
pray into the situation.

I asked the Lord to somehow confirm to me that these 'visions' were
God-prompted and that I wasn't 'leaning to my own understanding.'
The very next 'movie' was of a young lad with a motorbike. The
place was quite local to me. He was riding at tremendous speed
and negotiating a bend, but was travelling too fast. He skidded and
crashed the bike straight into a lamp-post, somersaulting from the
bike and landing on his back. I felt I was actually at the scene as it
took place and in my spirit I rushed straight over to him and tried
to take off his helmet.

I suddenly heard an authoritative voice say, "Don't do that because
his head is damaged." There was no one else around and I realised
that it was God speaking. I sensed I was back in my own bed, and
having done all I was directed to do for the young man, I was able to
relax and enjoy my sleep.

A long time after this 'happened,' we were invited to a church where
the Youth Group was conducting the evening service.

After the lively praise and worship, a group of young people were invited onto the platform to share some of their experiences whilst evangelising in Germany, including various street dramas they had performed. There was still some time to spare at the end of the proceedings and one youth encouraged another to share his testimony, because he nearly hadn't made the trip to Germany.

To my utter amazement, he began with the words, "I was riding my motorbike through a nearby town and couldn't manage the bend because I was travelling too fast." My ears pricked up. He continued, "My bike skidded, I hit a lamp-post and don't really remember anymore because I was knocked unconscious. Somehow though, I was aware of what I thought was an angel starting to take off my helmet and a voice saying firmly, "Don't do that because his head is damaged." He went on to explain what happened subsequently, but I wasn't hearing. My mouth had dropped open about as far as it could, and I was just staring at the young man as he recounted his story. I know I had asked the Lord to confirm that what I was seeing in the night was real, but this was mind-boggling!

This was about the only time that I had shared any of these 'visions' with my husband, and he was looking at me in total amazement.

Often we do not need to divulge things the Lord has shown us, but occasionally we need to step out in faith and say something, even if it seems totally ridiculous. When something is confirmed in such a spectacular way, we are encouraged and it brings great glory to God.

Chapter 7

YOU SHALL BE
FREE INDEED

BE PREPARED

THE IRISHMAN

EVEN THE DOG

VOICES FROM THE PAST

THROUGH THE WALL

SPIRITUAL WARFARE

A LYING SPIRIT

THE DARKNESS WITHIN

WHAT'S BEHIND IT?

BE PREPARED

'For the power of the life-giving Spirit has freed you through Christ Jesus from the power of sin that leads to death.' (Romans 8 v 2)

Years ago my husband and I used to help out as Advisors at various London Gospel Crusades. We were working together at Wembley one particular evening during a Billy Graham Crusade. For some reason I had a most unusual thirst and I left my husband for a while to go and find a drink. Aha! I spotted up ahead a group of stadium workers guarding the doors. "Where can I get a drink?" I asked. "Follow me" one man volunteered. It seemed that I was soon lost in a labyrinth of outer rooms and half-hidden doors which opened up into offices and much larger rooms.

Eventually we reached a long kitchen where other men were sitting on the worktops drinking what looked like stewed tea! I know I was thirsty but I *was* tested when offered some of the hot murky substance!

The men struck up conversation, questioning me interestedly about what I thought of Billy Graham's message. As I was answering there was a sudden BANG! Those of the men who were guards

Rebekkah Clark

leapt to their feet supposing that the preacher had been shot! They ran out towards the arena.

I tried to follow. I halted as I heard a woman's screams and turned to see that a group of people were trying to hold her down on a chair. She was wriggling furiously and struggling to be free. Prompted by the Holy Spirit, I went to offer assistance.

Medical staff had been summoned to attend her and were contemplating a sedative injection. They went off to get the necessary supplies.

The Holy Spirit guided me as to the real problem. I spoke to the woman, "You were in an air-raid shelter in the war, cowering from the noise and attack, and fear allowed a demon into your life. This terrific bang has triggered off the memory and with it the fear." (We learnt later that the noise had in fact been a violent thunderclap right above the stadium.) The woman allowed me to minister deliverance to her and I was able to see her set completely free.

The guards that had run to the arena had by now returned. The medical team had also returned complete with syringes. All were standing around watching what was going on. A doctor said, "I don't know what you are doing lady but, whatever it is, it is working." The woman became calm and soon was sitting quietly. It gave a tremendous opportunity to speak the gospel to all of these onlookers.

After what seemed an eternity, I arrived back at my seat and relayed the happenings to my husband. He had actually come to look for me and had seen what was going on. Knowing I was all right, he had returned to his seat.

A marvellous postscript. As Billy Graham concluded his message and invited people to come and find salvation some of those guards from the kitchen came forward to fill in decision cards.

So one woman being set free resulted in many lives being changed.

THE IRISHMAN

So if the Son sets you free, you will indeed be free.' (John 8 v 36)

I was at a Luis Palau Crusade in London and experienced in the deliverance ministry. There were not many that ministered in this field and counsellors would redirect people with this need to me.

At the end of one particular meeting I heard a loudspeaker announcement. "Could we please have a deliverance worker to come and help an Irishman?" At first no one moved, so I went forward. One other person then volunteered, encouraged by my response. "I'm a newcomer to this ministry, but I'm willing to learn and to assist you," he bravely offered.

We took the Irishman to the outer circle of the arena. We were quickly surrounded by a vicar (who had brought him to the meeting) and a large number of interested spectators. He didn't look very 'with it' to me. Help Lord! We were informed that he was the gang leader of a Northern Ireland paramilitary group.

He appeared to be drugged to the eyeballs and even seemed unaware that he had arrived in England – or how! He had been found on the steps of a church in London and the vicar had invited him to board their coach, which was just leaving for the Crusade. Isn't God's timing perfect? Somehow, he'd been put on the coach.

I have dealt with many such situations, but this had a completely new angle to it. "What to do Lord?" The Lord showed me that this man's spirit was floating somewhere out in the universe – outside of planet earth! I prayed and saw in my spirit where his own detached spirit was located. The Holy Spirit guided me as to what to say and do. Some of it sounded completely ridiculous. "Guide him to earth, bring him into the atmosphere, lead him across seas, deserts – and then take him to Israel!" I was instructed to lead him to Calvary and then to the feet of Jesus on the cross.

Never had I done anything like this before! I talked him through each stage of the process, and he identified with each one and responded. Step by step, returning to earth, his sanity was gradually restored. However, I sensed the man struggling to look up at the cross. I encouraged him to gaze at the nails in Jesus' feet, then to His pierced side and finally, he reached Jesus' face. This had been a great battle and it wasn't over yet. "Can you see the tears flowing down Jesus' cheeks? He is shedding them for you. Will you look into His eyes and see just how much He loves you?"

Slowly, the man looked into His eyes and immediately he came back into his right mind, just as the demoniac did who is mentioned in the Bible. Back from drugged oblivion to a state of normality. He was transformed!

The vicar and other onlookers were amazed and were still watching long after the rest of the stadium had closed. The vicar expressed the desire to learn and practice the ministry of deliverance. It is much needed.

The Irishman? He was saved, baptised in the Holy Spirit and spoke in tongues, although it took a few days for him to be completely set free. The vicar put him in the care of a special support group in another church, where he was nurtured and encouraged in his newly found Christian faith.

Some long while later I received a phone call from him to say he was going to be baptised by full immersion. He had not yet returned home, awaiting the right timing. Others of his previous gang would have killed him for desertion. A further six months then passed before he called to say that the Lord had now told him it was time to return to Ireland. He was now strong enough in God. He would tell his previous associates of his new found faith and he requested my prayer support.

I heard nothing further from this man. Sometimes we simply have to leave people in God's capable hands. I do know that a radiant, born-again man went home to Northern Ireland as a wonderful testimony of God's love and power to change lives. I understand that his story may have been told in a Luis Palau book.

God is no respecter of persons and He can do the same for you – whoever or wherever you are.

EVEN THE DOG

'When they arrived at the house, Jesus wouldn't let anyone go in with Him except Peter, James, John, and the little girl's father and mother.' (Luke 8 v 51)

The telephone rang. I heard an agitated voice announce, "My wife is in a coma. Can you come? The doctor says that she is unlikely to come out of it for three days." I agreed to call round, but first enquired as to the circumstances preceding this event.

Some time ago the man's wife had loaned to her brother a considerable amount of money when he was in great need, and this had not been repaid. She had never divulged this to her husband, fearing his disapproval. She then became a Christian and felt it right to tell her husband the truth but he was a violent man and had attacked her many times in the past, and so she was expecting a violent response.

Fear and tension had been mounting, but to her surprise her husband just shrugged his shoulders. Apparently this had been the cause of her drifting into a physical coma. I discerned this to be demonic and asked a couple who lived nearby to carry her into their own house. This would remove her from any immediate danger that might arise in her house, and afforded me more time to seek the Lord for guidance.

As I prayed, the Lord showed me those people that I should take along with me. More poignantly, the Lord also told me the people that were to be kept away despite being obvious choices! My husband (who was always a great prayer support) accompanied me to the house and we met the others there.

The man's wife was lying on the settee, still in a coma. Her husband was, by this time, naturally very concerned. The rest of the team had arrived and I shared with them what had happened and what the Lord was guiding me to do.

First of all, we on the team made our way to the wife's house. On arrival, we were greeted by a ferocious dog, fiercely guarding its territory. I looked the dog squarely in the eye and commanded it in Jesus' Name to lie down and be quiet! Immediately it slunk off and settled in its basket in the corner under the stairs and just watched what was happening.

I entered the downstairs cloakroom. The Holy Spirit prompted me to remove a picture of Jesus on the cross from the wall. We continued throughout the house, looking for any possible causes of demonic activity. We bound spirits in the house and prayed through every room and I gathered up some items as the Holy Spirit directed me. I had these, together with the picture, in my arms as we returned to the house where the wife was. Her husband spotted the objects in my arms and asked what I was doing with them. "I want to talk to you about these things," I said. "Is there anything in particular that I have here that you would find difficult to part with?"

"Yes," he answered, " That picture." This surprised me because there was no way that he could see that I had a picture among all the items in my arms. I knew then that this was the item that had a hold on him. "Go on," I replied, "Tell me more!" "Well, I go into the cloakroom quite often just to look at that picture," he answered. It seems he was mesmerized by it and had been deceived as it was a picture of Jesus on the cross.

Then I extracted the picture from the items that I was holding, and I told him to look at it from a different angle. As he did, he was shocked because superimposed on the picture was another image, that of a devilish figure and it was now clear that it was the picture's power that was causing havoc in their home. I sought permission to get rid of the picture together with the other items that I had collected and this was granted. Later we destroyed everything.

I then turned to the wife and took authority and bound every work of the enemy that had caused her to go into the coma. The enemy's power was broken from over her and she immediately opened her eyes and sat up!

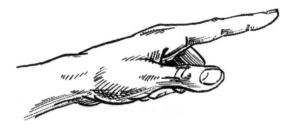

The next day she rang the doctor who was absolutely astonished that she was out of the coma so quickly. Another opportunity to witness that *anyone* can be completely set free!

VOICES FROM THE PAST

'Once when He (Jesus) was in the synagogue, a man possessed by a demon began shouting at Jesus.' (Luke 4 v 33)

As usual my husband assisted me and we were being greatly used in the ministry of deliverance. We were one of the deliverance teams of the church which we were attending at that time, and people came from far and wide for help.

On one particular occasion another husband and wife team were ministering with us to a man who had specifically come so that he could be set free.

It was then that I encountered demons from past ages for the first time. As we ministered he was firstly a squire from England and then a farmer from Ireland. The demons actually spoke in the voices of the characters they were representing. We prayed for this man, dealing with the voices from each era as they presented themselves, and eventually we saw him completely set free.

Perhaps the most unusual evening at this church was the occasion when deliverance had to continue outside on the steps of the building after starting inside, because the caretakers wanted to lock up. The lady being delivered was quite violent and screaming loudly and someone from the large crowd of onlookers called the police. Soon two police cars, sirens sounding, were racing to the scene, even coming up on the paved forecourt. When the policemen saw what was going on they quickly retreated, as some of their colleagues were church members, and all at the Police Station were well aware of the church's deliverance ministry.

THROUGH THE WALL

'Anything is possible if a person believes.' (Mark 9 v 23b)

One Saturday afternoon my husband and I were asked to go and pray in a certain house about fifteen miles away. The house was semi-detached, and the adjoining wall began to bother me. I felt a tremendous spiritual battle and forces coming against me from that wall. I moved over to it, laid my hands on it and commanded *whatever* was in the house next door to be gone by the morning. I did not know at that time what I was later to find out, but the Holy Spirit was leading my prayers.

 I learnt the next day that a nationally known astrologer lived in that house and that he had moved out that very morning. He had gone to live with his mother and a short time later he sold his house and moved away. The couple in whose house we had been ministering said that they had not known that he lived next door, and that they had been surprised by what I did when praying the previous day.

Some strange things had been happening in their home over a period of time and all was explained when they discovered who had been living next door. Now that the man had gone, the strange things that had happened in their house ceased.

Rebekkah Clark

SPIRITUAL WARFARE

'For we are not fighting against people made of flesh and blood, but against the evil rulers and authorities of the unseen world, against those mighty powers of darkness who rule this world, and against wicked spirits in the heavenly realms.' (Ephesians 6 v 12)

There was the time when a lady, whom I had helped, asked me to teach her about operating in the spiritual gifts of knowledge, wisdom and discernment. This I willingly did.

On one occasion I arrived at her house to find her looking quite troubled. "Can you please explain something to me?" she enquired. She then began to describe something the Lord had shown her in the spirit. It was her first experience of such a thing. As she continued, I was amazed. She was talking about a meeting between my husband and a business client. She had seen 'a knife hidden in the client's pocket' and had the distinct impression that the man had a murderous attitude. She believed he intended to use the weapon on my husband, with fatal effect.

She went on, "I prayed about it but the urgency didn't leave. I shared it with my husband and he prayed too. We agreed together in prayer until we felt a release."

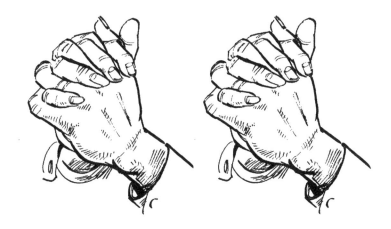

I enquired as to the date and time of this occurrence and later questioned my husband about it. It had sounded quite alarming. "Oh yes," he casually recalled. "The company has a very aggressive and fearful client that no-one relishes handling." And at that very time, my husband had been in a meeting with this client who suddenly was overtaken by an evil force and became very threatening, ballooning out, rising up to twice his stature and taking over a major part of the room!

My husband was unaware of any weapon but it had been necessary for him to bind the spirits in the client in order to calm him down. In fact this was the fourth time that my husband had had to do this with this man. On each occasion, when he bound the spirits in him, the man collapsed in his chair just like a balloon that had been pierced!

The picture that the lady had seen may have been a physical or a spiritual reality. We may not always have a complete understanding but it is important to move on what we have had revealed to us. In this lady's case, she and her husband had bound demonic forces from operating as they prayed in agreement together, even though they did not know all of the details.

The apostle Paul states in Ephesians 6 v 12 that our struggle is not against flesh and blood, but against authorities and powers of darkness in heavenly realms. Spiritual warfare is a serious matter. God seeks out those who are open to His promptings, who will listen and pray and who will allow themselves to be used in this way.

We all need to grow and learn from experience as we undertake spiritual warfare and only when we reach heaven will we know the effect of our obedience in this matter.

A LYING SPIRIT

'Instead of believing what they knew was the truth about God, they deliberately chose to believe lies.' (Romans 1 v 25a)

"Can you help?" This was not an unusual type of phone call. We sometimes received requests of this nature. The caller was from a local church that we had visited on several occasions.

I was somewhat reluctant when I learnt that those at her church were themselves hesitant to deal with the young girl as she was very troubled and had a compulsion to lie. The caller explained that there was no one else they could think of to ask, and that the girl was very desperate.

I eventually agreed to see her. I rang her and she invited me around to the house at which she was working as a nanny. She sat me down with a cup of coffee and seemed to be very much in control with a smug expression. I felt she was playing with me. The phone rang and she went off to take the call.

I saw her slip away to the bathroom to talk and heard the word 'mother' used quite angrily during the course of the conversation. I thought this odd, as her pastor had advised me that the girl had no living parents. When she returned I said, "You don't have parents alive, do you?" "That's absolutely true," she replied. I found out later however, that this was in fact untrue and that it was her mother with whom she had been speaking.

This young girl also had an obsession about the full moon and black cats. She said she was only able to sleep with her curtains open and the moon shining full on her face, with her black cat wrapped around her neck.

Tentatively I prayed with her and then rose to leave the house. I got into my car and the cat rushed out and jumped up at the partly opened window hanging on by its paws. It hissed and spat at me and its eyes were in full contact with mine. I realized I wasn't looking at the cat, but at a demon, which was trying to attack me! I felt quite vulnerable and had to deal with the cat right then. I spoke to the demon, "Leave in Jesus' Name." At that the cat slunk back to the house.

I saw this young girl at my house and prayed for her on many occasions after this incident. However, I only gradually realised how much I had taken on when I agreed to help her at the request of her minister!

I remember sharing strawberries and cream with her on one occasion, as we sat in the garden, and she told me about some of her difficulties. I opened my Bible and shared the Word of God with her. While I was reading to her she suddenly snatched the Bible from me and tore it in half. This tremendous strength could only have come from the demons within her.

She then ran across the lawn and up the side of a tree! I'd never seen anything like it ever before! I quickly took authority and spoke out in the Name of Jesus, while my husband held her down. She immediately came back into her right mind.

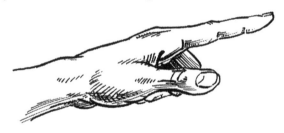

It took a long while for the lying spirit to leave as the girl quite enjoyed its presence in her life. Whenever she told us something and insisted that she was really telling the truth, it was a problem for us as we never knew whether or not she was still lying! My husband declared that a period of six months without a lie would be necessary to prove she had stopped lying and, only then, people could start to trust what she said.

She eventually knew complete deliverance from this and began to grow in her Christian walk.

Rebekkah Clark

THE DARKNESS WITHIN

'Create in me a clean heart, O God. Renew a right spirit within me.' (Psalm 51 v 10)

A young couple asked my husband and myself to come round to their flat and help them. They hadn't been married that long but were experiencing disturbing problems in their relationship. They thought there might be something wrong at their one-bedroomed home. It was small, with lounge and kitchenette.

I felt very claustrophobic as we entered but concentrated on activating my discerning 'antennae.' I asked if I might see the bedroom. There were certain things in there that no Christian couple should have had, things which would certainly not have been a help in their marriage. They readily agreed when I asked the couple to relinquish these.

I returned to the lounge and my eyes were drawn to their records and some art volumes. I would not normally have been quite so particular but the Holy Spirit prompted me to enquire about one of the records, one completely unknown to myself. It belonged to the husband and again he was more than willing to part with it.

The art volumes also grabbed my attention. They were beautiful, antique, leather-bound books which had been handed down to the wife as family heirlooms. She was, of course, reluctant to let them go when I mentioned them.

Up to this point, I had not looked at any of the books, but there was a tremendous sense of darkness and evil emanating from the area where they were sited. Hence, I scanned them, but apart from pictures of the usual nude women, I could see no reason for this sinister feeling. I quietly talked to the Lord about it and He directed me to place one of the big volumes (24 x 12 inches and 4 inches deep) on the floor and He would show me.

Before our very eyes the book opened and we were confronted with extreme evil. The wife was horrified. She asked, "Does the whole book have to go or is the evil perhaps just contained within a few pages?" It was agreed that we would tear out only two pages and my husband and I took them home with us to burn, along with other occult books and records that had also been found. We had an incinerator in our garden especially for this purpose.

Back home, it was midnight and my husband and I burnt the books and records first. Then we put in the two pages but noticed that they would not burn. Suddenly, a gust of wind came from nowhere and caught away the two unscathed yet charred pages. They rose up into the air and came to rest in the garden two doors away.

We retrieved them and put them back into the incinerator, this time taking authority over all demonic influences and commanding those pages to burn in the Namc of Jesus. The most horrendous scream came out from the pages and we stood there to ensure that every last bit was destroyed and that every demon had been sent to the rightful place where it belongs. We prayed that the neighbours would not have heard, nor had been tuned in to those supernatural screams.

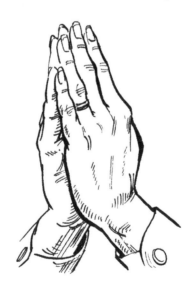

The next day we received a call from the young couple. "Have you destroyed everything because things seem to have got worse for us and we are still under attack?" I asked the Lord, "What did I miss?"

I sensed that the husband had taped a copy of one of the records. When we went round to their house, I confronted him and he was aghast. He thought he had got away with this and had deliberately tried to deceive me, also having copies of some of the other records too. The husband was very repentant and destroyed all of the tapes in front of me.

The original request was to help sort out problems in their marriage. The matters dealt with at this time were all against marriage commitment and a good, healthy relationship. A few other matters were dealt with on subsequent visits, and the couple went on to enjoy a very happy marriage, being blessed with children.

Footnote
It is my experience that many occult things that come into Christian homes are gifts from other people. The sentimental attachment sometimes makes it hard to relinquish them but it must be done.

I was once visiting the home of a leading Bible teacher when a parcel arrived from his sister for his birthday. When he opened the gift, it turned out to be an expensive porcelain ornament, something, however, that no Christian should have in his home. He had a choice to make and he made it instantly. He asked his wife and myself if we agreed with what he was about to do, which we did. All of a sudden he let the ornament slip through his fingers and it broke into pieces when it hit the floor!

This may seem extreme to you, but this man had a ministry and a family to protect. This was more important to him than offending his sister or allowing the value of the ornament to affect his decision. We must not let *any* detestable thing into our homes, even if we risk offending the donor when they visit!

WHAT'S BEHIND IT?

'No longer will anything be cursed. For the throne of God and of the Lamb will be there, and His servants will worship Him.' (Revelation 22 v 3)

A single mother told me she was experiencing problems in her life. As I waited, the Lord clearly showed me that there was an evil influence connected with the wedding ring she was wearing. It turned out to be antique and had belonged to her grandmother. I prayed and broke any curse from that ring and then the mother was able to keep it.

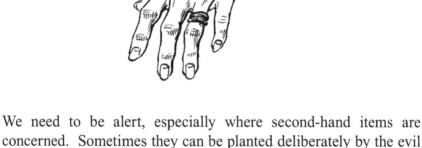

We need to be alert, especially where second-hand items are concerned. Sometimes they can be planted deliberately by the evil one. I emphasise how important it is to believe the Word and to pray for discernment.

A friend saw an ouija board in a charity shop window. She offered the shop assistant some Christian books in return for it and the shop assistant agreed. My friend immediately went home and destroyed the ouija board to prevent anyone else from being able to buy it.

Some things are obviously evil, whereas other items are good in themselves but may have had a curse or negative pronouncement made over them. We all need discernment in order to identify these and in deciding how to deal with them.

.

Chapter 8

USING THE GIFTS

OUT IN THE OPEN

THE GIFT OF FRIENDSHIP

THE RING THAT HAD TO BE REMOVED

RUNNING AND LEAPING AND PRAISING GOD

NOT THE FINAL WORD

THERE'S JUST SOMETHING ABOUT THAT NAME

WRONG ARM OF THE LAW

SNAKE ALERT

ONE DAY IT WILL BE TOO LATE

OUT IN THE OPEN

'A number who had practised sorcery brought their scrolls together and burned them publicly. When they calculated the value of the scrolls, the total came to fifty thousand drachmas.' (Acts 19 v 19 NIV)

My husband and I had been invited to the house of a couple who had recently become Christians. They were having difficulties in their relationship and wanted us to pray with them. They had been involved in many evil things before their conversions and had to destroy a number of things that they had accumulated in their lives.

As we began to pray, a picture came into my mind. It was of something like a box-type briefcase, inside which I saw a syringe and drugs. When I questioned them, the husband answered, "No, no, we don't do that stuff anymore," as he turned to his wife.

The Holy Spirit impressed upon me, "It's in the cupboard under the stairs." I relayed this to the couple. The husband said to his wife, "It sounds like your case, but I thought you got rid of it?" I emphatically reiterated that it was still there and insisted he take a look. He looked in the cupboard and there it was! It was exactly as I had described. The wife then admitted that she had kept it, but now agreed that it should be destroyed. It is pointless trying to hide or deny things in your life and still expect to progress in the Lord. Progress won't happen until such things are dealt with.

Not destroying such things gives the opportunity to be tempted back into whatever a person has been delivered from.

We continued to pray for healing in their relationship. The wife was gifted in art and brought out some of her drawings for me to see. They were all of herself, beautiful drawings, but they were depicting a person in despair. These gave more information for us to pray as the Holy Spirit led us.

In due course both of them were used mightily for the Lord.

THE GIFT OF FRIENDSHIP

'A real friend sticks closer than a brother.' (Proverbs 18 v 24b)

I once asked the Lord to give me friends that were like-minded spiritually and I was surprised how soon He brought the first friend into my life.

My husband and I were driving to church one Sunday and I sensed the Holy Spirit instructing us to go to a church in completely the opposite direction, in fact in another area. I shared this with my husband and he agreed to turn around and go there.

By the time we arrived, the service was already under way and so we slipped in quietly, and we were given two seats at the side. It turned out to be a baptismal service and a beautiful young lady stepped forward to take her turn to be baptised, her lovely long hair twirled up on her head. Looking radiant, she stepped down into the water and the Lord clearly gave me a picture for her. I didn't know if it would be in order for me to speak out and so I raised my hand and asked the pastor whether I could do this. "Certainly," he replied.

I spoke to the lady, describing how the Lord had showed me that life is like a garden, with many seasons and stages of growth. I seemed to be looking through an elongated line of arches, beyond each there was a square garden. The first garden was overgrown with weeds, thistles and harmful stinging nettles. "You don't have to stay there," said the Lord to the young lady. "Anytime you are ready, you can walk through the arch into the next stage of your life."

The next garden contained ground that had been toiled and broken. Then she went through another arch to another garden where the ground was ready to receive seeds. God showed that the Holy Spirit would water those seeds and that as He did so, small green shoots would spring up. The Holy Spirit continued to water and then the Lord invited her to go through the next arch.

She walked into the most wonderful fragrance, a garden enriched by colour and every kind of bloom imaginable. A seat was there for her to pause and enjoy such a rich and lavish aroma. It was as though the very presence of God was invading her every sense.

Now she had learnt to rest but He beckoned her on and she walked through yet another arch into an orchard. She had no idea what the trees were because there was no fruit as yet. First the buds and then the leaves were to be formed, and then would come the fruit. She watched this happening and God was saying to her, "If you keep walking with me you will produce beautiful healthy fruit that will last forever in My Kingdom."

The lady smiled up from the baptistery as I gave her this picture. After the service had ended she came to talk to me and to say thank you. She introduced me to her husband and two little girls. Something clicked from that moment onwards.

Although she has lived in many different places, even abroad, there has been a bond that has not broken and we keep in contact. I now see that this picture has been fulfilled in her life because she has borne amazing fruit in her life for God.

Her husband and children who at that time did not share her faith subsequently became Christians and joined her in serving the Lord faithfully.

THE RING THAT HAD
TO BE REMOVED

'So no one can become my disciple without giving up everything for me.'   (Luke 14 v 33)

A group of people brought a woman to our church and asked our pastor if anyone might be able to help her. He directed them to me. The woman was completely unknown to me and seemed to be suffering from a mental disorder. I needed the Holy Spirit to help me tackle this problem.

I noticed that she was bedecked with jewellery – in her ears, around her neck and a ring on every finger. The Holy Spirit instructed me to ask her to remove the necklace. She was *very* hesitant but eventually complied. Unbeknown to me, the removing of that item broke a spiritual bondage from the woman.

Then I sensed that the Holy Spirit wanted me to focus on a particular ring on one of her fingers. The mere suggestion that she take off this ring sponsored a violent reaction! It took some time to calm her. I tried another ring on a different finger. She avoided eye contact, but seemed quite happy for any other item to be removed, except the one that I knew needed to be removed.

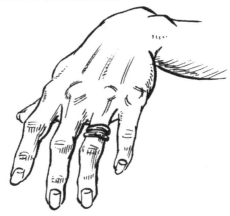

Rebekkah Clark

She had a friend with her who had been ministering to her over a period of time, and I explained to the friend that I believed the Holy Spirit was showing me that this particular ring had a direct association with the mental difficulties she was encountering and that she would be set free as soon as the ring was removed from her. The friend's pleading was to no avail. She would not remove the ring and the woman was later admitted to a mental hospital for a period of between twelve and eighteen months.

Some time after this, I was in a nearby village and I saw this woman walking towards me. She was in her right mind and in the company of the same counsellor friend. She bounded towards me smiling broadly, looking really pretty and radiant. How different from the depressed and dishevelled figure I had previously encountered. I almost hadn't recognised her!

After a fond greeting, I invited them for coffee, during which time the woman explained that throughout her stay in hospital, thoughts of the ring had continuously crossed her mind, an inner voice prompting her to take it off. However, as time went by, her friend who had faithfully and regularly visited and prayed for her, noticed that all of her jewellery had been removed with the exception of *that* ring.

Then one day the woman was 'twiddling' with the ring and her friend asked her if, once and for all, she was ready to take it off. Although she was still not of sound mind and not able to reason coherently, yet, suddenly, with an act of her will, she clasped the ring – and pulled it off! Instantaneously, she stood up, completely sound of mind. Her friend then led her to commit her life to Jesus Christ.

This was the woman I was now beholding. What a transformation! God alone knew what was associated with that ring and what had held the woman in such bondage and had so dramatically affected her life for so long. God alone knew how to bring about her deliverance and salvation.

Praise His wonderful Name.

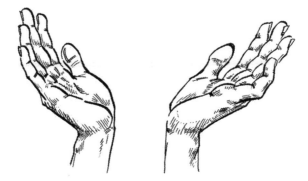

RUNNING AND LEAPING AND PRAISING GOD

'He jumped up, stood on his feet, and began to walk! Then, walking, leaping, and praising God, he went into the Temple with them.' (Acts 3 v 8)

Some friends from our church once held a series of Healing Meetings, open for anyone to attend for ministry.

I had not been involved with any of the arrangements and didn't know where the meetings were being held. My husband and I felt prompted by the Holy Spirit to attend and so we drove off, asking the Holy Spirit to guide us each step of the way. We sensed when to turn right or left at each junction and eventually arrived at our destination. Those leading the meeting were very surprised to see us and concluded that God had obviously wanted us to be there!

During the meeting, a boy who could not walk was carried in. We prayed and laid hands on him and just praised the Lord as we saw the boy jump to his feet and run around the church.

How easy it would have been to simply have turned the car around and gone home and so miss the meeting and then we would not have had the joy of seeing the fruit.

NOT THE FINAL WORD

'Who is able to advise the Spirit of the Lord? Who knows enough to be His teacher or counsellor?' (Isaiah 40 v 13)

Life's never dull in our house. There was the time when my husband rushed off to a hospital in order to rescue his aunt. As if severe heart problems weren't enough, her condition had now been worsened by a hospital bug! My husband's mercy dash brought her to our house, where she could be nursed back to health.

That night however, she looked so unwell that I rang my own G.P. who kindly came out to see her. His verdict was that she was close to death and would not live until the morning. His advice? "Pull the sheet over her head but don't phone me until the morning!" Somewhat less than optimistic don't you think?

My husband and I were praying that evening before retiring to bed, when what I call a 'righteous anger' rose within me. I just *knew* it wasn't her time to die as yet she did not know the Lord and I was *not* going to allow the devil to take her life prematurely. Purposefully we went into her room and following the leading of the Holy Spirit, laid hands on her, praying authoritatively in Jesus' Name, that she be healed by His stripes. We then went to bed ourselves.

The next morning she was alive and certainly beginning to recover. How? It's always a good sign when someone shows an interest in eating, and she asked for a boiled egg for breakfast! This was the first food that she'd taken for some while, and she managed to eat the yolk.

The next day she chose to try a little fish. Every day saw her body and life being gradually restored and strengthened with the nourishment she was receiving.

By way of a footnote, we were meeting in our lounge with others one particular Sunday to praise and worship the Lord and take communion together, when, quite unexpectedly, my husband's aunt walked down the stairs to join us! Over the years she had heard the gospel message, but now wanted to find out more. The result was that she gave her life to Jesus. She was in her late seventies at the time and lived for a further six years.

Doctors *don't* always have the last word!

THERE'S JUST SOMETHING
ABOUT THAT NAME

'So that at the name of Jesus every knee will bow, in heaven and on earth and under the earth.' (Philippians 2 v 10)

The car packed, we set off on our journey home.

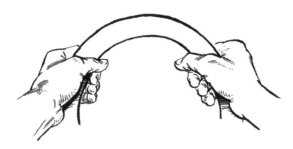

It had been a marvellous holiday in lovely Cornwall and we were reluctant to leave. My husband was driving the car, skilfully negotiating the narrow country lanes. This was still part of the holiday for me, and I was enjoying the beautiful yellow gorse on either side.

Gazing around as I enjoyed some music, I was suddenly alerted to a car heading towards us at terrific speed, and on *our* side of the road! It was about to collide with us and my first natural instinct was to grab the steering wheel from my husband and try to turn the car off the road. He appeared not to have seen what was happening at all! Instead, I cried out "Jesus!" Instantly the car heading towards us vanished!

On questioning my husband afterwards, it seemed that he had noticed nothing out of the ordinary and we realised that this had been a demonic attack in an attempt to drive us off the road and kill us. Praise the Lord that at His Name, *every* knee must bow and we were protected under the shadow of the Almighty, in whom we believed.

WRONG ARM OF THE LAW

'Get away from me, Satan! You are seeing things merely from a human point of view, not from God's.' (Mark 8 v 33b)

My church was about fifteen miles from home and on one occasion I had been teaching at their Bible School. I was chatting in the car park afterwards to a friend before we went our separate ways. After a while I noticed a police car parked on the other side of the road, just ahead of us. For some reason, I discerned all was not well and I suggested that my friend get into her car and drive home quickly.

I prayed her on her way. I thought it strange; although we had been outside talking, neither of us had noticed the police car arrive and park. I made my way to my own car and felt I wanted to get home as soon as possible.

I drove along the inside lane of the motorway, but realised that I needed to move over into the middle lane if I were not to be filtered off with the exit-lane traffic. It felt safer and more open in this lane as it was by now almost midnight and very dark. There was no traffic in front or behind but I was suddenly conscious of a police car right behind me with its blue light flashing. Where had that car suddenly appeared from? The police driver was indicating that I should pull over on to the hard shoulder. I was reluctant to do this because I remembered that recently a young girl had been murdered on the motorway when her car had broken down.

Yes, we all have to face faith challenges at times. It *was* a police car, and I *know* I was supposed to obey, but I sensed that something was not right. I was not going to open the window and in fact locked my car with the central locking as I pulled over into the lay-by. The motorway was empty of traffic and I was shaken by the sudden appearance of a face at my passenger window. Although a policeman in uniform, his eyes seemed full of evil.

I was ordered out of the car, but in my spirit I sensed something very wrong. I asked the Holy Spirit for guidance and felt I should stay put. The policeman insisted I lower the window, but I called out to him with all the wisdom and bravery I could muster, "I will meet you at the local police station." My engine was still running and so I indicated to leave the hard shoulder. I looked across at the passenger window and to my amazement, the man had gone!

There was no police car behind me either! As I pulled out onto the motorway, mine was *still* the only car around. I drove straight home and told my husband all that had happened. Did this happen because I had been speaking on 'Deliverance' that evening?

The next day I rang my pastor and relayed the events to him. He fully believed my story and recounted a similar occurrence that had happened to him.

SNAKE ALERT

'As Paul gathered an armful of sticks and was laying them on the fire, a poisonous snake, driven out by the heat, fastened itself onto his hand.' (Acts 28 v 3)

When my husband and I were first married, we volunteered and went to the mission field. We found we were living in the jungle not too far from an American community. This was quite an oasis but it did emphasise the vast contrast of lifestyle in the area, either extremely poor or extremely rich.

One day we were trying our hand at some golf with a few of the Americans from that community when a small, green, tree snake fell on my head. It then slithered down my body. (We had been trained how to react to pythons and cobras and knew how long we had to reach the emergency services should there be a need. In fact we had been taught to stand perfectly still in just such a scenario.) This snake however, was apparently the most poisonous in the jungle and had it bitten me, I would have died instantly.

I was a Christian and had to bring every thought captive to Jesus! I didn't want the adrenaline in my body to entice an attack from the snake.

The onlookers seemed quite amazed as they stood back and watched the snake slide down me and slither away in to the jungle. I was then able to witness to them that this was my God looking after His child and answering prayer.

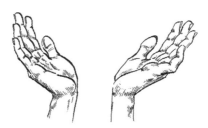

ONE DAY IT WILL BE TOO LATE

'For God says, "At just the right time, I heard you. On the day of salvation I helped you." Indeed, God is ready to help you right now. Today is the day of salvation.' (2 Corinthians 6 v 2)

The phone rang. How many times does the phone ring in each day for mundane reasons? This time however it was an emergency call. It was the hospital. A close relative of mine was unconscious and in a protected room.

We raced to the hospital and were told what had happened. My relative had gone into hospital for an X-ray for a back problem which required an injection of blue dye, a routine procedure but this had gone horribly wrong because a dirty syringe had been used on him. He had accidentally been infected with the meningitis virus and was apparently now near to death!

We were taken to where he was but we could only see him through glass windows. I stood and prayed, knowing that I had taken the opportunity to talk to him about God's love on many previous occasions. He had always refused to make any decision, joking that God could catch him on his deathbed – after he had lived his life!

Sometimes it's better not to gamble over such matters, especially when they have eternal consequences. Here he was on that brink of death. Had he had time or thought to pray that prayer and given his life to Jesus? Would we ever know, this side of heaven?

God is so gracious. Our prayers for healing saw a gradual improvement. We were eventually allowed into his room, clad with masks and overalls to prevent further infection.

When he was awake and able to talk, I found out that he still had not given his life to Jesus. This could have been his last day on earth. This could have been his last chance! He did not take it and he could have been lost forever.

FINALLY

If this book has challenged you to tap into your God-given potential and you are encouraged in any way I would love to hear from you, especially if you have prayed the prayer for salvation.

Please send an E mail to rebekkahclark@btinternet.com

Also if you have any interesting accounts that you wouldn't mind being put into a future book please let me know.

Suggested prayer for becoming a Christian.

Dear Lord Jesus,

Please forgive my sin and for the way I've lived my life until now, for doing things my way and not yours. I now take you as my Saviour and my Lord and I will endeavour to live for you day by day from now on.

Thank you for dying on the cross so that I might be reconciled to you. I now hand my life over to you so that you can take control.

Please forgive my selfish and sinful ways and I turn to you for help and guidance.

Thank You Lord Jesus.
Amen.

REBEKKAH CLARK was brought up in North West London, England, the middle child of three, with an older sister and a younger brother. She became a Christian at the age of eighteen and met her husband shortly afterwards. They have three daughters and seven grandchildren.

Rebekkah has had a singing, speaking, counselling and deliverance ministry and, with her husband, has served on the mission field, has helped pastor churches, has served as an Adviser in national evangelistic crusades and currently is helping pioneer a small growing church in the south of England.